Advance praise for *This House Is Not a Home*

A crucial and intimate story that unpacks the devastating truths of the past and current crisis faced by displaced Indigenous Peoples.

It intricately moves through three generations living a traditional life, to land dispossession, and the inspiring recovery of a family determined to return and reclaim the beloved territories of their ancestors.

This House Is Not a Home singularly captures the legacy of Canada's colonial agenda to rid the land of Indigenous Peoples and the fallout that ensues.

— Brandi Morin, author of *Our Voice of Fire*

Absolutely exquisite. Told with such love and gentle ferocity, I'm convinced *This House Is Not A Home* will never leave those who read it. I am in awe of what I've witnessed here. Mahsi cho, Katłı̨à. Bravo!

— Richard Van Camp, author of *The Lesser Blessed* and *Moccasin Square Gardens*

Just finished your book. It is wonderful, Kat! Enlightening and touching! Miigwetch!

— David Bouchard, author of *We Learn from the Sun*

This House Is Not a Home

This House Is Not a Home

KATŁĮÀ

Roseway Publishing
an imprint of Fernwood Publishing
Halifax & Winnipeg

Development and copyediting: Kaitlin Littlechild
Text design: Jessica Herdman
Cover design: Ann Doyon

Printed and bound in Canada

Published by Roseway Publishing
an imprint of Fernwood Publishing
2970 Oxford Street, Halifax, Nova Scotia, B3L 2W4
and 748 Broadway Avenue, Winnipeg, Manitoba, R3G 0X3
www.fernwoodpublishing.ca/roseway

Fernwood Publishing Company Limited gratefully acknowledges the financial support of the Government of Canada through the Canada Book Fund and the Canada Council for the Arts. We acknowledge the Province of Manitoba for support through the Manitoba Publishers Marketing Assistance Program and the Book Publishing Tax Credit. We acknowledge the Province of Nova Scotia through the Publishers Assistance Fund and Arts Nova Scotia.

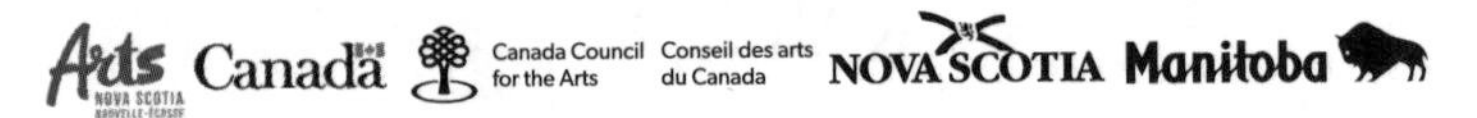

Library and Archives Canada Cataloguing in Publication

Title: This house is not a home / Katłıà.
Names: Lafferty, Catherine, 1982- author.
Identifiers: Canadiana (print) 20220263078
Canadiana (ebook) 20220263086
ISBN 9781773635620 (softcover) | ISBN 9781773635835 (EPUB)
Classification: LCC PS8623.A35776 T55 2022 | DDC C813/.6—dc23

For my children,
May you be as strong as the ancient rocks at your feet,
yet as gentle as a resilient northern flower,
and may this contrasting beauty surround you
on the land that calls you home.

PROLOGUE

Before the public housing system entered the Northwest Territories, many Indigenous Peoples lived off the land in canvas tents, teepees and log cabins, but when housing was introduced, families were divided through the separation of households and a new way of living was introduced. This lifestyle change caused a further loss of culture for Indigenous Peoples other than the enforced methods of assimilation into colonialism such as residential schools under the Indian Act.

Many Indigenous Peoples were accustomed to living together in close quarters with close and extended family members, aunts, uncles, grandmothers and grandfathers. Government housing policies call this overcrowding, but if we look closer, it's actually a part of a larger support system whereby families come together to help each other, where everyone has a role to play.

Today, many of our Elders live in old folks homes on the outskirts of the community, rarely visited by family, often passing away much earlier because of the loneliness and depression that overcomes them. Young people are losing their cultural traditions, including language, because their Elders are not in the household to help parents take care of the children and pass down teachings with wisdom, patience and guidance.

Men rarely hunt and woman rarely gather or harvest and prepare meat like before because our lands have been encroached. Society says we should leave the old ways behind and work for a living to pay bills, something that my ancesters never had to worry about when living on the land. When they did try to find work in the days of forced assimilation, they often had a hard time because of lack of access to proper education and workplace discrimination, and their strengths were on the land. They became labelled as idle because they had a hard time getting hired and often had to rely on social assistance. This is the cycle that many Indigenous Peoples have become trapped in and often resort to other means of income, sometimes illegal, to survive. However, with globalization, efforts like Idle No More and land back are gaining significant support as Indigenous Peoples resist government power and control and assert our inherent Aboriginal Rights and Title. Indigenous Peoples are collectively rising up as the rightful stewards of the land that we have lived on since time immemorial in order to once again live a more sustainable, harmonious, unified lifestyle in line with Indigenous law like our ancestors once lived.

INTRODUCTION

I was inspired to write this story when I learned of a family that I know that had been living in poverty within the housing system for many years in the Northwest Territories, Canada. Before housing came into their small Dene community they lived in a small shack by the water. They did not have running water or electricity, but still, they had everything they needed.

Once a year they would set out on a hunting trip where they would be gone for a couple of weeks. They left most of their belongings behind and took only what they needed for surviving out in the bush. It was a beautiful event that the family looked forward to.

But when they returned from that hunting trip they came back to a vacant, empty lot where their humble shack once stood, with all their personal, irreplaceable belongings gone with it. Their home had disappeared. The family started frantically asking around the community about what had happened to their home. They were told that the housing corporation had come and assumed they had abandoned their home, and as such, it had been bulldozed to the ground.

This family then lived in a tent for the next year with nowhere to go. Eventually, in its place, the government built a boxed home with running water, electricity and appliances and told them they could live there if they paid rent. They had no choice but to move into the new housing unit because they required shelter for the coming unforgiving winter months.

This took place in the late 1980s. Since then, this family has had a strong resentment towards the government. They have difficulty keeping up with their bills because they do not have a formal education. Their knowledge was on the land and still is; they never had to rely on making money to live. To this day, this family continues to struggle — living in poverty and never getting the justice they deserve for what happened to them.

This family and many other families across the North had to involuntarily give up their homes for something that was considered a better way of living by the same government that imposed their policies and beliefs, denying the principles and laws of traditional Indigenous ways of knowing. In this way, housing is a direct infringement of Indigenous Rights and Title.

With government cutbacks, many of the houses that are currently listed as public housing units in northern communities are in major need of repairs, and they are riddled with mould, which makes people sick. Although there is a declaration on the rights of Indigenous Peoples to live in safe environments and suitable housing conditions, this treaty is being broken because it is not binding.

Because of scenarios like this, and many other similar stories, the mindset of some Indigenous Peoples living in housing today is that they shouldn't have to pay to live on their own land. Many Indigenous Peoples are reclaiming their land, connecting back to their traditional lifestyles of living off the land and asserting their rights as part of reclaiming their cultural identity in an assertion of land back.

I am a domesticated creature of colonized habit
I don't know how to wield an axe or snare rabbits
Yet today I am going out for a drive on the highway to find
a new place to call home
Somewhere past the reservation zone
Yet not too far because I'm scared to be alone
I am settling in somewhere between urban and wild
I am freeing myself of society and acting like a disobedient child
I will not settle on the money man just because he might know how
to help me survive
I will know when I'm home again
When I feel reclaimed and alive
Whether this home I build be in the form of a mansion or a shack
I will stake my heart on the land and never turn back

CHAPTER 1

Kọ̀ was taught that every animal had a reason for being, but he had great difficulty understanding the purpose of the mosquito. Letting one of the annoying buzzards land on his exposed, balmy skin, he watched the pesky insect curiously. Why was its long stinger designed solely for the purpose of drinking blood? Kọ̀ wondered. Without consent, the insect took as much as it could carry and flew away, low to the ground, heavy with the weight of Kọ̀'s sticky red blood, leaving a cruel itch and a large welt in exchange. Not a fair trade at all, Kọ̀ thought.

It was early morning, still dark, but Kọ̀ and his father were already on the move. Kọ̀ tried to sit still and quietly like his father, but he was restless. Their backs upright and straightened against a towering cold piece of flat slate, they waited for the perfect opportunity to approach the large bull moose they had been following closely for the past day and a half.

Kọ̀ was born in one of the most unforgiving parts of the world. In a place where the cold can kill a man in a matter of minutes. Where one wrong move could end a life. Where there is no room for mistakes, no room for doubt, no room for anything other than survival. Where at the end of the day gratitude sets in. A deep appreciation to Creator. Having lived now for the count of ten winters, Kọ̀ was thankful to be alive each and every day and grateful for all things Creator made.

Kǫ̀ learned from a young age not to let one day go by without giving thanks to Creator. To Kǫ̀, Creator was the land, and the land was Creator. They were one and the same. For thousands of years, Kǫ̀'s family travelled the vast North. They had many gathering places that spread far and wide in all directions. They knew the best spots to pick berries and where to set traps. They knew where to lower their fishing nets and which migratory routes the caribou would take from year to year. The land was their home. They had many homes. Some areas they travelled to for the summer, other places they would hunker down for the long winter. They had no need to stay in only one place; the entire countryside was theirs to explore. Kǫ̀'s ancestors passed on the knowledge of the land and how to live as one with the land from generation to generation so as not to lose their way of life.

Kǫ̀ developed a sense of pride in knowing how to survive on the land with his heart and his hands, mostly through the teachings of his father. Because of this, Kǫ̀ learned to both love the land and fear it for he knew nothing was as powerful as nature, and for that he respected it greatly.

Kǫ̀ studied his father's serious weathered face as they sat together in wait. He couldn't remember the last time his father had spoken other than giving him short orders. His father had no need for words; one look from him told Kǫ̀ all he needed to know. On the land, words had little meaning. Words were weak sounds carried away by the wind, but actions had strength behind them.

The rare time Kǫ̀'s father did speak was when he told stories, stories that Kǫ̀ could not entirely piece together all at once. Kǫ̀'s father was a good storyteller, but Kǫ̀ was often left with many unanswered questions.

"Ts'ehwhı̨̀." He was assured by his mother that, in time, he would come to know the ancient teachings in the stories and the meaning behind them, that he would one day be the one to tell those same stories and pass them on to his own children. Everyone Kǫ̀ knew was a storyteller. They all told stories with lessons behind them. Stories were told incrementally, throughout the years, so that the message would become ingrained in the listener, retained for life after an entire lifetime of repetition.

Kǫ̀'s father started in on one of his stories to pass the time as they sat in the reeds near the mouth of the river at dusk, their two hidden figures blending in perfectly with nature far downstream from the rushing waterfall, in a quiet place where the river lapped into a calm stir. The cascade still towering over them from afar. It was no question to Kǫ̀ that the moose was alive just as much as he was. It lived and breathed. And although beautiful, it was very dangerous. If one were to get too close, one would surely be taken under by the sheer force and power behind it, his father warned. "Hojı." It continuously created its own storm, the rushing current dancing together night and day endlessly.

"Ejìecho eyıts'ǫ hòezıʔejìe deh nąìlı̨ łak'a ts'ǫhk'e negı̨̀hʔà ı̨dè, ekò dè asìıdeè goxè ładı̨ agode ha." His father stared out at the waterfall in the distance as he told his son one of the oldest prophesies he knew. It was said that when the two animals, the bison and muskox, from different parts of the land meet on either side of the waterfall it would be a sign of great changes to come.

Kǫ̀ had passed by that very same waterfall countless times when he accompanied his father on his fall hunt. He had always admired it knowing it was an important landmark. This time though, as his father painted the picture of the two large brutes at the top of the waterfall in his imagination, he looked up at the high cliffs that encased it in astonishment, admiring the falls from a new perspective. He imagined the great creatures standing at the foot of the cliffs looking at one another, ready to fight or maybe to make peace — he wondered. Kǫ̀ would never look at the waterfall the same again without hoping to catch a glimpse of the two powerful animals.

The prophesy of the muskox and bison would eventually mark a change in the life that Kǫ̀ lived, his father continued. "Ekìyeh nı̨dè, gòet'ı̨̀ı̨ ɗıı neèk'e nàgede gıgha dezhì agode ha." His father's words struck deep and gave Kǫ̀ a pang of panic he'd never felt before. He didn't want to believe it. To not be able to live on the land was unfathomable to Kǫ̀, and he forced the thought from his racing mind, happy to be distracted by another small swarm of mosquitoes drawn to the sound of his fast heartbeat and hungry for blood. When one of the bloodsuckers landed on the back of his hand, his reflex took over and he flattened it before it had a chance to take from him. He hoped it would set an example to the others but they were relentless.

The tanned moose hide wraparounds and red fox fur collar that Kǫ̀'s mother made for him blended in with the red, orange and brown autumn leaves that he covered himself in head to toe to blend into his surroundings, hidden from the moose they were tracking.

When Kǫ̀ and his father hunted, they never came back empty-handed. They would be gone for days, sometimes weeks, only to return home when they were successful. To go home empty-handed was the unspoken failure of a man. One moose was enough to feed and clothe their small family for a season, more than that, and they would share what they had with the community. Through giving and taking, Kǫ̀ was taught that all parts of the animal were equally important and never wasted; if not used for food, the animal would be used for clothing and tools.

Kǫ̀ grew more and more restless as they waited in the reeds for the moose to enter their range. They had been calling and waiting all day, exchanging the tried-and-true mating ritual through their mimicked moose calls knowing it was only a matter of time until the moose would come into view. Moose hunting was still a steep lesson in patience for Kǫ̀. It was difficult for him to sit still for he was still too young and full of energy, not like his father who seemed to have all the time in the world, napping in between moose calls or praying to Creator, Kǫ̀ couldn't be sure.

Kǫ̀'s eyes grew big when he finally saw the smooth brown body and large antlers that looked like old brittle bone walk out into the open. He tugged quietly at his father's sleeve. He knew better than to speak but couldn't help it. "Dendı," he whispered. Kǫ̀ scrambled to a kneeling position to get ready to jump up quickly into a run, but his father held his arm out in front of him using the universal sign to be quiet by putting his finger to his lips.

Not knowing its end was near, the large animal walked directly in front of them towards the water, dipping its large front hoofs into the crystal-clear lake. The bull moose took a long look at the view of the great waterfall in front of him before lapping up a much-needed drink. Kǫ̀ watched and wondered in awe if the animal was capable of admiring the beauty that it was born into or if it didn't have a mind to think apart from its own survival.

Kǫ̀'s father collected himself and slowly crouched onto one knee raising his bow and arrow in wait, giving the bull a chance to finish its long-meditated drink. As sure as the winter nights are dark, the animal took its time, almost as if it knew it was going to be its last sip. Through the trees, Kǫ̀'s father closed one eye and pointed the scored end of the arrow directly at the magnificent creature as it turned in their direction to make its way out of the water.

The bull's ears flinched from the faint sound of the million-year-old stone, the sharpened edge already on its way, travelling with a sharp zinging sound that could be heard over the crashing of the distant falls. Spinning sharply, the slate punctured the moose right below its left ear on the thick, folded skin of its neck, yet it wasn't pierced deep enough to slow the large beast down entirely and the moose turned and ran in the opposite direction, its instincts kicking into full force.

Kǫ̀ was already on the move, trailing closely behind the animal and well in front of his father. He splashed through the water, his feet barely skimming the surface, his knees high in the air to gain more speed. He took a shot with a smaller version of his dad's arrow without taking a moment to aim only to meet with the animal's rear. Not slowing it down in the least, the bull reared its front legs up for a moment and splashed down into its wake and ran even faster. Not quite the target Kǫ̀ had in mind. He broke the dry spruce bow in half over his bent knee, angry at himself for missing his chance at proving he was a skilled hunter.

Kǫ̀'s father had already situated himself on the other side of the shoreline, correctly assuming how the scene would play out. Facing the animal head on, Kǫ̀'s father fearlessly stood in front of the ramming bull waiting for it to come to him knowing it had nowhere left to run.

Kǫ̀'s father raised his bow and arrow looking the animal directly in the eye. Giving up before the kill shot, the animal did not carry the look of fear; instead it had a look of surrender as if it had already accepted that its time had come. It slowed to a stumbled trot, no longer looking around for an escape, the slight wound in its neck set in and it fell into a kneeling position as another arrow pierced through the tender part of the animal's side between its large rib cage, the kill shot. With its lung punctured, blood flooded its diaphragm, ultimately causing the creature to suffocate. Out in the open, under the setting sun, the mighty dendı had no other choice but to face its end; the great animal had met its fate.

Blood spilled out in one long steady stream from its puncture wound in the same way the waterfall fell to the earth and the bull sank into the shallows of the river on its good side. With one of its antlers sticking straight out of the rocky bottom, it rested on its chin, its gullet sweeping in the stream. The blood from the bull discoloured the mirrored shallows until the lake turned into a swirling deep maroon around its nearly lifeless body.

Without hesitation, Kǫ̀'s father walked quickly towards the moose and drove his long carving knife straight into its thunderous heart to be sure that it would not suffer any longer, for the animal still had its spirit and deserved dignity.

Kǫ̀'s father pulled a handful of tobacco from his satchel as Kǫ̀ slowly caught up to where they were. Crushing the dried flakey leaves in his palm, his father gave some to Kǫ̀ to spread on the ground near the animal's antlers. Kǫ̀ studied the horns that were as big as him, pieces of them chipped from its many battles. Their edges were sharp but every curve was full of soft fuzzy velvet. Kǫ̀ realized then just how much they curiously looked like moss and lichen. Kǫ̀'s father closed the moose's watery brown eyes and gave thanks to the animal for giving its life over to them for their needs.

Together Kǫ̀ and his father made a fire near the shoreline and worked well into the night skinning and cutting the moose to prepare the carcass for the long journey home. They were careful not to puncture the full slippery stomach as they worked to remove the kidneys and liver. They removed its limbs first and pulled out its ribcage by cutting a handle in between the bones. With the spine left lying parallel to the ground, the head and the hide were the only things left remaining. They cut into its still warm flesh and separated the sticky thin webbed membrane from the layers of skin and fur. The nose was removed by holding onto the top lip above its rectangular white teeth and cutting around it with a small sharp blade. The heart was as big as Kǫ̀'s head, and he held it carefully with both hands when his father handed it to him to place it down carefully. It was a tedious job with enough work for ten men, but they were more than skilled for the job and their stone blades were sharp.

This was the life that Kǫ̀ knew. It was the only life he knew. He didn't know what the world was like outside of his hunting and trapping grounds. He couldn't know that in another part of the world a different way of living existed, nor would he have paid any mind as it had no impact on him either way. He was content. His bed was made of thick rows of soft spruce bough, the only thing separating him from the cold hard ground at night. Being that close to the earth, his dreams were always good and vivid, the energy in the ground reinvigorating him throughout the night to give him the strength he needed to endure another day of hard work.

Kǫ̀ found comfort in the familiar sounds of the birds waking him in the morning with a song he could easily mimic with his whistle. A whistle that was only for the day, not at night, or it would bring unwanted spirits under the light of the dancing northern lights.

Kǫ̀ enjoyed the distinct smell of the different flavours of smoke that each tree gave off when burned in the fire, comforting him with a warmth that started in the pit of his stomach and slowly filled his entire being with contentment.

In the summers, Kǫ̀ spent most of his time on the banks of the lake on one long stretch of narrow rocky shoreline in the shadow of a promising lookout point where his mother would pick berries. The peninsula was the place he most resonated with what a home was. It was most familiar to him as it was where his family always returned to once the weather warmed. It was there he often sat and watched the glorious pink sun sprawl across the landscape after a long day spent helping his mother cut and hang fish to dry.

The sun hung high in the air on those long summer nights, and he found it particularly hard to sleep when the weather warmed. In fact he hardly ever slept at all in summer since the midnight sun did not sleep either. During the peak of the warm season, when the North became hot and dry, Kǫ̀ missed the winter. To find some temporary relief from the heat, he would jump off the high cliffs and into the frigid lake, swimming laps with the jumping grayling in the shadier areas near the shore.

In the winter, when out on the traplines with his father, he would catch snowflakes on his tongue to ease his thirst and pass the time when his father wasn't looking. Wherever he was he always had the open sky to guide him. He made up his own fun and games. Never bored, he would test his balance by looking up and standing on one foot under the blanket of stars melding together with the fluffy snowflakes that sprinkled down on him in the light of the fire glow, making him feel like he was flying through the night, reaching heights so high that nothing could ever bring him down. His life was uncomplicated, and he never suspected that it would ever change.

CHAPTER 2

The seasons came and went, and before Kǫ̀ knew it, he had grown tall enough to meet his father at eye level. It was finally his turn to go it alone. To show that he could provide for his family and the family he would one day have.

It took more time than his father would have liked, but Kǫ̀ had learned the art of patience. He had been waiting for his turn to go out on the land alone ever since he saw his older cousin make the trip. When Keeweetin returned, there was something different about him. He looked the same, but he had changed. He seemed taller, wiser. He no longer wanted to play childish games with the other kids; he was more interested in sitting with the Elders and listening intently to their teachings. Kǫ̀ wanted what he saw in the change in his cousin and couldn't wait for his turn to go out on the land alone.

It took some time but eventually Kǫ̀ had proven to be a skilled hunter. He had taken down a pregnant calf that very summer and gave the fetus of the ekwǫ̀ to his Kookum as is customary without having to be told how to prepare it for her. This pleased his father and ultimately sealed his fate; he would be the next young man in the community to journey alone and show his family he was fully capable of surviving out in the tundra.

When the day that Kǫ̀ had been waiting for finally arrived, the dogs could sense they were soon to be put to work. Commotion was in the air with the preparations for Kǫ̀'s journey, and they were more excited than usual, wagging their tails in a frenzy; they were anxious to hit the trails they knew so well. Kǫ̀ didn't dare show his enthusiasm. Even though he wanted to howl at the moon like the dogs, he was reserved, acting mature on the outside in front of his father but on the inside, he was just as riled as the dogs to be going on one last long haul before the end of winter. This time he would guide the dogs on his own; he was ready to take the reins.

Kǫ̀ loved his dogs. He took pity on them whenever food rations were low. He would save scraps of meat for them after mealtime and sneak out to feed them late in the evening after his parents were asleep. The dogs soon came to expect Kǫ̀ would feed them whenever they spotted him around the corner of the house from their fenced-in dens at night. They would start in a low whine that grew louder and louder in a sad rhythm until they were in a full-blown howl. His dad would sometimes shoot him a curious glance, wondering why the dogs' ears always perked up and their tails wagged when Kǫ̀ was in sight, but he would just shrug his shoulders.

The dogs were only with Kǫ̀'s family during winter. In summer, all community dogs were rounded up and brought out to a small island a half day's travel from the peninsula where they would be visited every other day for feedings. It was easier to contain them that way and less of a disturbance when they started on one of their collective drawls.

The night before Kǫ̀'s journey, white clouds of breath circled above the dog team and hung in the cold open air as they jumped over and over looking up at Kǫ̀ in a wild fury, nearly breaking free of the ropes that held them down. Kǫ̀ tried to hush them; he would get in trouble if his father found out he was giving them more than they needed. They were kept lean so they would be in the best shape to break trail. Their hunger was a tool to keep them going. It was the food that was used to fuel their energy during the long haul. Like dangling a piece of meat, they were given small portions to keep them wanting more. The dogs were built to be light on their feet but strong enough to keep going in the worst of conditions with their heavy coats and ice-blue eyes that matched the northern sky.

In the morning, Kǫ̀'s father led him down a trail to the edge of a small, frozen pond. "Tı welǫ̀ ts'ǫ̀ tambaà welǫ̀ ts'ǫ̀ anede eyıts'ǫ ts'ıh dehshe-le neèk'e ts'ǫ̀ anede," he said, giving him directions to follow the shoreline and keep going until he reached the place where the trees don't grow. It was the same place he had gone every year with his father. Kǫ̀ was confident that he could find his way with his eyes closed but he listened to his father; he would stick to the trails and follow the stars if need be. "Tı̨lı k'e zǫ anet'ı̨. Ets'ǫǫ̀neètła nı̨dè, edàanı̀ whǫ̀ dàele wenàowo hoghàneètǫ sı̀ı weghà nàı̨̀da." Kǫ̀ nodded and cracked his whip on the ground next to his dog team and the hounds took off in a roar. He held his head up high, already taking in his independence without looking back at his father, who had a slight look of worry on his face.

Making his way steadily towards the place where the land divided and the tree line would become a backdrop, it would take Kǫ̀ a few days to reach his destination. He was to keep going until the land opened up to a blank canvas that stretched out for what seemed like an eternity until it met with its love, the ocean.

Kǫ̀ forged on, putting hundreds of miles of distance between himself and his family. The environment around him became bleaker the further he went, the wind stronger without the shelter of the trees. He ran his dogs steadily across the invisible lines embedded in the rock shield drawn across the land by Creator's hand, separating the landscape into different scenes. Every time he travelled the tundra it was like discovering another world.

He knew he had made it to his destination when he spotted random boulders scattered unevenly over the land. A clue left behind by the massive glaciers, broken down into smaller pieces and dragged along a slow encapsulated frozen journey of time, thawing and melting for what might have been eons. When the ice eventually disappeared altogether, sporadic large, lonely boulders dotted mysteriously in the middle of the endless open countryside for the odd arctic fox or rabbit to hide behind when trying to escape from predators.

When Kǫ̀ stopped and looked all around him, he could see just how far from home he was. The few trees were sparse and reduced to tiny shrubs as tall as his knee. Old paw and sled imprints ran parallel to him every which way in the snow but he did not encounter any travellers, nor did he expect to in the vast surroundings. He got to work quickly to build his shelter for the night when he found the clearly visible stone structures called Inukshuks that mapped certain landmarks, the only other sign of human life to be found for days in between camps. The Dene shared the land with Inuit, who lived mainly along the coastline. Kǫ̀ was told by his father to go no further than the Inukshuks and he listened. Once he spotted the familiar markings of the statue-like rock formation in the distance high upon a rock mound, he stopped and looked around for a place that would be sheltered from the winds. He found a small mound of dirt and snow, a "pingo," his father called it, a term he learned from his encounters with their northern neighbours.

There Kǫ̀ and his dogs stopped for the night. Kǫ̀ tied up the dogs and got to work building his quincy, a small igloo-like dome that he made by piling snow in the shape of a large circle with his hands until it was compact and up to his waist. As he waited for the quincy to harden, Kǫ̀ worked hard to chisel out holes in the frozen overflow for drinking water. After a few hours he hammered sharp wooden stakes in as far as they would go. It took him the day but he managed to pack down the quincy until it was solid, then he shoved a few dozen twigs into it, no more than the length of his wrist to his elbow, all around the roof.

He stood back and laughed, seeing that it looked almost like a giant porcupine. He waited a few more hours for the snow to bind together to form a strong ceiling, then he started in on the entrance, making sure it was facing the pingo so no wind would get in. From there he began carving it from the inside out until he reached the tipped end of the sticks. This left just enough room for him to shimmy in feet first on his stomach and sleep.

And sleep he did. Kǫ̀ never knew such solitude, such silence, but even in his isolation, he was not afraid. The fresh open air in his lungs helped him breathe a deep and satisfying breath and he slept peacefully tucked in his furs, sheltered from the gentle winter winds without a care in the world.

Kǫ̀ woke early and prepared to head for home. He wasn't quite ready to leave the beauty of the tundra but wanted to make good time to show his father that there was no reason to doubt him any longer.

It was still early morning, and Kǫ̀ had been making good speed as he headed for home, but when a loose jagged rock no more the size of a robin's egg jammed in his lead dog's paw, Kǫ̀'s troubles were only just beginning. The pebble rolled underneath the dog's paw in such a way that it caused it to buckle under him and break. Denah'ke tripped, steering the sled too far to one side; Kǫ̀ gripped the sled harder, cracking his whip beside the dogs to get them back on course. Kǫ̀ shrugged it off but after running for quite a ways on a broken paw, Denah'ke could go on no further and came to a gradual stop, with the rest of the dogs having no choice but to follow his pace. Again, Kǫ̀ cracked his whip on the ground and hollered "hoòh," not understanding why his team was coming to a complete standstill. Only when Denah'ke started to whimper and lick his paw did Kǫ̀ realize something was wrong. He ran to Denah'ke but the dog didn't want Kǫ̀ near and jerked away. Kǫ̀ got on his knees to inspect his paw but Denah'ke's incessant scrambling only served to make things worse and he tangled himself in the reins of his harness, causing the dogs behind him to pounce and bark in urgency.

Kǫ̀ tugged at the other dogs' harnesses to stop the chaos and scolded them to settle down as he slowly reached for an anxious and scared Denah'ke, petting his head to calm him. Denah'ke whimpered and shook, trying to stand but falling down every time. Denah'ke's paw was weak and hung at his side. Running on it steadily had injured it even more.

"Shhh," Kǫ̀ whispered as he smoothed Denah'ke's head over and over, trying to calm him while also looking around trying to figure out what to do next.

Kǫ̀ took off Denah'ke's harness and used all his strength to carry the unwilling dog to the sled, lowering him in on top of the oversized mat of rough muskox wool he had folded in the bottom.

"Įzhìı̀," Kǫ̀ said, pointing for him to lie down. Denah'ke just looked up with saddened eyes. The dog was reluctant at first and tried to jump out when he saw his predecessor at the lead, realizing he was no longer needed. "Įzhìı̀, Denah'ke!" Kǫ̀ shouted again for him to lie down in a more forceful tone for Denah'ke's own good. Denah'ke had no choice but to take Kǫ̀'s orders and he lay whimpering in the front of the sled, his eyes straight ahead. The team continued along but at a much slower pace; even with a broken paw, Denah'ke was faster than all the other dogs.

At the rate they were going, Kǫ̀ was beginning to doubt that they would make it to the tree line before dark. When the sun quickly set, he knew he would be spending another night out on the tundra, which meant that most of what was left of his wood rations for fuel would have to be burned. A cold chill ran through Kǫ̀ knowing he could freeze to death if he ran out of firewood, but he didn't give in easily to his fears; instead he calmly humbled himself to Creator, remembering all that his father taught him.

Kǫ̀ kept going until the last ray of sunlight disappeared behind one long wall of snowdrifts shingling the landscape to the west of him. It was there that Kǫ̀ had no choice but to set up camp for the night. He built his shelter under the tallest drift he could find, which offered some protection from the wind. He would try to get some sleep before heading home in the early morning while it was still dark to make up for lost time.

Before retreating to the dream world Kǫ̀ tried once again to have a look at Denah'ke's paw. The break needed to be bandaged to prevent Denah'ke from putting any more pressure on it. If not his running days would be over, and Ko's father might think it best to put him out of his misery well before his time.

Kǫ̀ softly brushed the top of Denah'ke's front leg and patted his head until he settled down and lay still. Eventually, Kǫ̀ was able to slowly bring his hand down to Denah'ke's paw. He lifted it gently and had at the ready a blunt from a piece of his kindling supply, which he placed across the bone to prevent Denah'ke from stepping on it any further. Kǫ̀ quickly wrapped it tight to hold the splint in place and Denah'ke let out one long drawn-out howl as Kǫ̀ tied a firm knot.

As if the unforeseen turn of the events hadn't already made Kǫ̀'s journey difficult enough, the loud sound of Denah'ke's pain-filled drawl was heard in the not too far distance by a curious and hungry pack of wolves that had been following them since they first heard Denah'ke cry out in pain. The pack began mimicking Denah'ke's cries; only their howls were not of pain but of hunger, giving reason for Kǫ̀ to not let his guard down. He tried his hardest to stay awake all night to protect his dogs, but the events of the day and the fresh air defeated his senses in the dead of night, and he fell asleep sitting upright next to the fire. When he woke, Kǫ̀ and his dogs were surrounded by more than one set of deep glowing eyes, lighting up the dark, ready to attack as their glistening drool flickered brighter than the dwindling fire before Kǫ̀.

Kǫ̀ jumped to his feet, gripping his knife in one hand and throwing the rest of his wood supply into the hot coals with his free hand to bring up the flames and scare them away before they came any closer but the wolves were relentless. They scavenged what they could from Kǫ̀'s food rations, moving like ghosts in and out of the light. They weren't about to stop until they got what they came for after sniffing out a weak and injured Denah'ke.

Kǫ̀ yelled, "Nąìtłe," trying to fend the hungry pack off in vain as Denah'ke, too, tried to fight them off but was unable to protect himself from the predators for long. Kǫ̀, being as small as he was, was thrown down to the ground and only able to fend off one of the wolves as the rest made off with Denah'ke, the wounded one barely limping behind.

Kǫ̀ stayed ready to defend himself for the rest of the night long after the wolves dispersed. He cried out of anger, trying to hold back his sobs as he shook. The dogs got no rest either; on edge, they huddled together closely under the dark night sky, their bodies twitching them awake every so often. Kǫ̀ sat in what was left of his sled and held onto the reins hoping the wolves wouldn't come back for the others. There he waited desperately for the light of day.

Come morning, Kǫ̀ went through what was left of his diminished food supply. With Denah'ke gone and his sled nearly destroyed, Kǫ̀ wished his father was with him now more than ever; he didn't know how he could go on any further without his help and guidance.

With one side of his sled now torn down from where Denah'ke was pulled out and what was left of his firewood rations gone, burned in the fire in Kǫ̀'s hapless attempt to fend off the wolves, Kǫ̀ thought of what his father would do if he were in the same situation and knew he had no choice but to keep moving. And so, Kǫ̀ began to do what he could to fix his broken sled to get himself to the tree line. He turned the collapsed sled onto its good side and cut some of the leathery stripped willow off his whip to pull through the holes in the paper-thin dried caribou skin, threading it to rig up the sled to the point where it could hold in his salvaged belongings so nothing would fall out on the long ride home.

Next, he untangled the reins and lined them up for the long trip ahead. Without a doubt, Kǫ̀ knew he wouldn't last another night out in the open. He needed to make it to the tree line before dark but the weather took a turn for the worse once they set out, testing Kǫ̀ and his dogs even further.

The sudden ruthlessness of winter blew over the open landscape with a ferocity that Kǫ̀ never knew possible. An eerie wail crept deep down into Kǫ̀'s lungs and ribcage as the oncoming blizzard danced unceremoniously around him and his dogs, causing the exhausted team to look back at him as if asking to stop and rest. But Kǫ̀ kept them on their feet, fearing the worst if they were to stop in the height of the storm but at the same time fearing he might push them to their limit if he ran them for too long.

He cracked his whip steadily as he rode into the wind. He kept his head down to protect his face from the hard sleet that stung his eyes, feeling more like tiny shards of glass. He looked far beyond his years as he hunched forward into the wind, leaning heavily with his elbows onto the sled handles to keep himself from blowing away.

It didn't take long for the storm to fully encapsulate Kǫ̀ and his dog team, and it was as if they had suddenly found themselves at the bottom of a mountain caught in the rush of a rolling avalanche. The dogs were the first to disappear, then all at once, Kǫ̀ could no longer see his own hands as he held them out in front of him. Nearly snow blind, he put all his trust in the dogs, that they would know to stay on course, but it wasn't long before their original trail was out of sight. The sled slowed to a near stop, the front of it stuck knee-deep in snow. Kǫ̀ jumped off to try and readjust it as the dogs tried anything, even swimming, to get above the powdery snow.

Kǫ̀ looked around for the trail but it was no use; it was long buried. He searched and searched desperately for any small sign of the way home but had no luck. His knees buckled from the pressure of having to trudge through the deep snow that packed under his feet as he walked. Using up all his energy, he couldn't go on any further.

The trail was completely hidden under the large snowflakes that blew sideways in the wind, dampening him from head to toe. Kǫ̀ couldn't see them, but the dogs looked to him, their faces apologetic as even they shivered through their thick fur.

Kǫ̀ remembered what his father told him. "Whǫ̀ weghà hoghàd̨ıtǫ." He looked up to find his way, but even the sky looked out of place. The clouds were so close and dense that he could feel the pressure of the low ceiling in his temples, making them throb. He tried to find the formations that he knew by heart. He put his hand up and closed one eye to measure, but his view was clouded over every few seconds by the fast-moving clouds. His eyes sopped with snow, leaving his vision blurry and his lashes frozen and stuck together. He closed his eyes for a few seconds and cupped his hands, breathing into them to let the heat from his breath melt the fast-forming icicles that settled heavily onto his eyelids, but it was no use, the snow clumped together on his lashes mere seconds later. He needed to find shelter and fast.

Kǫ̀ spun around, looking up in a dizzy. He was lost and the only thing he found was the fear that he might never find his way home. It was a possibility Kǫ̀ had never entertained, but to panic was to die, and so he stopped spinning and started to pray to Creator for guidance.

When his fluttering heart slowed to a steady pace, he opened his eyes and saw the sun breaking its way through the clouds, giving off just enough light for him to see something big and dark a few yards away. A lone bison. Kǫ̀ had never seen a bison before but to him it looked similar to a muskox, yet unlike its mammoth relative, the bison didn't belong that far north. Kǫ̀ thought he was seeing things until the dogs started barking at it. The bison was covered in just as much snow as Kǫ̀ and his barking dogs. Steamy snowflakes gripped its long brown beard. When the snow became too bothersome it huffed and shook the crusted snow off.

No sooner had Kǫ̀ spotted it than the bison turned and walked away, vanishing into the drifts of snow that formed thin sheets of ice in the air. Trusting that he had been sent a spirit guide, Kǫ̀ followed in search of answers. He quickly reached into his sled for his snowshoes, strapped them on his cold feet and followed the burly animal, leaving his worried dog team behind.

Kǫ̀ tracked the animal a good way but when he looked back at his own tracks he knew he would have to stop following soon or he would lose his way back to his dogs altogether as they were quickly being buried by layers of falling snow. When he was just about to give up and turn around, the bison walked to the top of a steep hill and bowed its head low to the ground shaking its beard free of snow once again. The animal seemed almost ethereal as Kǫ̀ crouched below, nervously waiting for it to make its next move, careful to keep his distance in case the animal wasn't mild mannered.

Taking in a big breath of air, the bison let out a short gruff snort before gathering speed, as if getting ready to charge, and bolted powerfully down the hill and out of sight once again.

Kǫ̀ hardly had the energy to scramble over the small hill to see where the bison was headed, but when he made it to the top, he could see the faint outline of the tree line in the distance, and to his relief he saw the small gap between the trees indicating a well-used trapline. The trail. The bison came to an abrupt stop before meandering the rest of the way on through the cut line without looking back.

Kǫ̀ found his way back to his dog team who had, by then, made themselves comfortable beds insulated by the snow. Cold and wet, Kǫ̀ crawled into the sled and covered himself head to toe in his carpeted muskox fur for shelter, careful not to let any air get in. He desperately wanted nothing more than to get home to feel the warmth of a fire, but he knew he could not run the dogs any further in the blizzard. He worried that they could be stranded for days if the storm did not let up, but it was better to have seen the trail and not be able to reach it rather than not finding it at all Kǫ̀ thought.

Inside his blanket of muskox fur, Kǫ̀ curled up in a sitting position hugging his knees with his head between his legs. He shivered uncontrollably and jumped awake every time his chin fell to his chest until he was too tired to fight sleep and his head bobbed until morning.

Kǫ̀ woke the next morning with an immense surge of hunger but he could hardly move to help himself. His body temperature had dropped significantly in the beginning stages of freezing to death even though he felt warm. He had seen it once before when he and his father and some of the other men in the community went searching for one of their relatives who hadn't made it home for some time after going out alone to check his traps in an oncoming blizzard. His clothes were scattered along the trail from removing them one piece at a time thinking he was warm. They found the man lying dead and naked on his back next to a tree. When they lifted him up Kǫ̀ had to look away. The skin down his entire backside had turned the darkest shade of purple from frostbite.

With the storm over, Kǫ̀ felt like he was in the middle of the summer heat, but he knew better than to start removing the layers he had on. The image of the dead man had traumatized him so much that he hugged his muskox fur even closer around his shoulders noticing then that it was covered in Denahk'e's blood. He promised that he would burn it in honour of Denah'ke if he ever made it home.

Sometime during the night, the snowfall had dwindled to light flakes and the morning the sun was trying to peek through what was left of the storm clouds. Kǫ̀ found himself missing his mother's cooking. The thought of eating a piece of marrow and bone broth created a small drop of drool that dripped down the side of his mouth.

Once he found the strength to move, one by one he helped the dogs out of the trench of snow that was built up high on either side of them, blocking them in. He had to make sure not to break a sweat for he knew that it would turn his body to ice.

Kǫ̀ and his dog team somehow haphazardly made their way to the tree line before midday. With his food supply wiped out by the wolves, his stomach screamed. He thought about getting to work setting traps. He hoped that he might get lucky and catch a rabbit, but the rabbits were scarce that year. Kǫ̀ knew it was the reason for the wolves' attack and he didn't bother to waste his time trying to set snares. Besides, his hunger was so fierce that he needed something immediate so he resorted to digging through the snow at the base of the trees in search of frozen berries.

When his hand met the hard cold ground, he grabbed a handful of dirt and twigs digging his nails into the earth until they hurt. To his relief, he found a few sparse frozen blueberries in the mix. He held them in his hand and brought them close to his heart thanking Creator. Too impatient to wait for the berries to thaw, he tucked them into the inside of his cheek to melt them down and in one gulp he was able to curb his hunger just enough to dig for more.

With the small provisions, his stomach was no longer empty and he managed to catch a few camouflaged ptarmigans sitting on a low tree branch next to him by throwing the muskox fur over top of them and fed them raw to the dogs. He watched as they fought over the small white birds tearing them to pieces feathers and all.

On the last trek home, the snow from the night before had hardened in the bright sunshine and Kǫ̀'s sled glided easily over one long sheet of slippery sleet. A warm wind was at his back helping to rid him of the chills from the cold sweat he had tried to avoid, the last of winter now behind him.

When Kǫ̀ returned home, a great feast followed. His father nodded at him with a confident look, as if to say he never once doubted his son's ability to survive alone. His mother was brought to tears when she heard the sound of the bells hanging off the dogs' harness running up to the house. He had arrived much later than expected but all the same, he had arrived.

Kǫ̀'s mother ran outside hugging her white rabbit fur shawl that she always had wrapped around her shoulders and held Kǫ̀ close, combing down his sweaty hair with her hands. He was almost too embarrassed to hug her in front of everyone; after all, he was now a man and shouldn't need his mother. Still, as he held back his tears, he was thankful to feel her warm embrace.

Kǫ̀ didn't feel all that different then, but he knew that something within him had changed. He now had a story to tell; he could survive on his own.

But Kǫ̀'s glory was short lived. The missionaries were making their way north by boat and what he now knew of survival would take on a whole new meaning. It would take a different kind of strength to come back from the place where he was going.

CHAPTER 3

The first thing they did was change Kọ̀'s name.

He stood in line with other children his height not knowing why he was being shuffled around, but he would soon learn that this was just the first of many unpleasant introductions to the atrocities of the school. Staring straight at the back of another child's head in formation, he didn't know he was second last in line to go into an empty white room to have his long dark hair dunked in a barrel of kerosene and cut uniformly like every other child in the lineup.

The women in charge all wore long black dresses but one woman in particular, not much bigger than him, was armed with a long rod that she hit over her hand repeatedly to scare the children into submission. Kọ̀ thought about running but was too frightened to move. When the woman reached him in line, she hit him hard with her long rod over his shoulder and asked him harshly, "What's your name boy?" She grabbed him by the ear and shook his entire head violently when he didn't answer right away.

Kọ̀ didn't speak English, but he understood what she was asking when the other children in front of him had belted out their given names. After an older child asked them what their name was in their language. She had already learned some English having been at the school for a time and translated for them.

Forcing his name from him he yelled "Kọ̀" in hopes that it might stop the madwoman from pulling on his ear but the woman still swatted him on the back of his head in one hard sweep. Kǫ̀ didn't know what hurt worse, his head, or his heart. He wanted to rub the throbbing pain away but he was too afraid to show even the slightest weakness so he kept his arms straight and stiff at his side. "From now on you'll be called Christian," she informed him sternly, pushing him forward in line to exercise her authority over him and show that she was in charge.

The change of name was especially confusing for Kǫ̀. What he knew of names was that they were chosen thoughtfully, and often well after a baby was born. The Elders would watch a child's behaviours, learn their character. When a name was given to a child, a feast and naming ceremony would take place. Kǫ̀ vaguely remembered the day he was named. His relatives packed into his family's tent and sat on the ground sharing a meal. Everyone hugged him, tousled his hair, his aunties squeezed his cheeks. Kǫ̀ knew what his real name meant. It was given to him by his great-grandfather, and he was told that one day he would honour it greatly, but now all he could do was miss the meaning behind it. It was there at the school that they would try to turn him against his own family, ridicule his culture and make him forget everything he knew.

The line moved slowly, brutally until all the children were given a new name in English. Towards the end of the line, the nuns ran out of ideas and the children's names became repetitive. Every other child was named the same as the next and numbered to avoid mix up.

The attempt to obliterate their identity did not stop at their names. The moment Kǫ̀ arrived at the school he knew that something wasn't right. The large brick building was hard, cold, closed in and unforgiving. All his senses felt confined. Instead of spending most of his days outside, he was barely able to go out at all.

At night, sleep evaded him. The hard, creaky metal cot was far from what he was used to sleeping on. He missed the cradling ground, the fresh smell of pine, the crackling of the warm fire, the sound of the wind blowing outside his tent. Now all he could hear were children sniffling in their beds. He closed his eyes and imagined a storm coming in so fast and strong that it would rip the roof right off the school and float them all up and out of there.

Sometimes Kǫ̀'s spirit would leave his body. On his ascent back home, he would look down and see from above all the beds placed in perfect order in the middle of a large open room. The women, who he learned were called nuns, took turns walking up and down the halls hushing the children and hitting the headboards to scare them into keeping quiet. The violent sound inevitably ushered Kǫ̀ reluctantly back into his body.

Kǫ̀ held fast to hope, expecting that his father would come barging through the doors at any moment. His father would come and rescue him, he was sure of it. It was only a matter of time, but after Kǫ̀ lost track of the days, his hope slowly diminished and turned to an inward numbness.

In just a few days at the school, Kǫ̀ dramatically lost weight. He didn't have much stored fat on him to begin with but within a short period, he had been reduced to being able to touch his thumb and pointer finger around the very top of his arm. His muscles were relaxed and tender to the touch, no longer hard. His protruding spine at the base of his neck was noticeable when he was told to kneel and pray. Whether it be at the long dinner table or church, his bones showed through the plain loose clothing that he had no choice but to wear day after day.

He didn't know that he was withering away by refusing to eat what the nuns were serving; all he knew was that he would rather go hungry than eat what was given to him. Having grown up on a diet that mainly consisted of fish, he knew what fresh fish was supposed to taste like. The fish that was served to him on a plate was not only full of bones, it was rotten and covered in maggots after having been left out on the back steps of the schoolhouse long after it was caught.

One day, after another boat load of children had arrived at the school, a child began to choke on a fish bone and was yanked away from the table. Kǫ̀ didn't see him again after that. It wasn't uncommon for flies to land on the children's food, and at times larvae would be swimming in the oats, but if food was refused the strap came down hard on the backs of necks.

Some were force-fed to be made an example of. Kǫ̀ was no exception. His face was smashed into a piece of foul-smelling fish until he couldn't breathe. Later he was scrubbed with a wire brush until his skin bled, "to get the stench off" the nun would say as if that made it acceptable.

With all of this, Kǫ̀ wondered why his father had not come for him yet. His fists and heart became permanently balled up and tense. Why would his parents allow him to be here? He tried to push the thoughts out of his mind and tell himself that they could not know the terrible things that were going on or his father would have already saved him. His parents would never allow him to be treated with such disrespect. Surely if his father knew something wasn't right, he'd do everything in his power to get Kǫ̀ out of that awful place. He would not only help Kǫ̀, but he would also save all the other children and bring them home to their families too. If he only knew.

Kǫ̀ clearly remembered the day that he was taken. His father had gone out to check his trapline a few days before. It was one of the rare occasions that Kǫ̀ didn't go with him. He needed to stay home and help his mother with some of the chores around the house as she wasn't feeling well.

Kǫ̀'s mother was inside preparing food. Kǫ̀ was outside, as always. Sitting on a boulder. Happy to have his chores finished, he was curled over a small piece of wood that he was chiseling into one of his many carvings that improved with each piece of wood he dedicated to the craft. He had just finished carving out the eyes of an eagle when he saw something from the corner of his own eyes.

Boats were slowly making their way through the communities on the peninsula, stopping at every house along the shoreline. When the strange people got back into their canoes there was a commotion followed by faint cries and people huddling together. He couldn't make out what they were saying but knew something wasn't right and ran to tell his mother.

Kǫ̀'s mother followed him outside to see what was going on but she stopped in the doorway of their house and leaned on it for support, holding her stomach when she saw what was happening. The two of them watched as it became apparent that the canoes were slowly filling with children, children being dragged away from their parents as they tried to hold onto each other, not knowing why they were being torn apart.

Kǫ̀'s mother took him by the hand and hurried him inside and shut the door. She continued about her business, preparing their next meal as she always did. When Kǫ̀ tried to ask her what was happening, she didn't respond. Kǫ̀ saw his mother trying to hide the fear on her face. It was as though she didn't want to know what was happening, as though she didn't want to accept it. With a look of disbelief, she closed her eyes to try and keep her tears in and will the missionaries out, but Kǫ̀ could hear their paddles cutting madly through the water as they came closer.

Little did Kǫ̀ know that his mother had got word some time ago that the missionaries might be headed north. Her cousin had learned of the strange people from her husband's brother, who had gone as far as the flatlands to trade. Their relatives in the south warned of people dressed in costume who were travelling to the communities and who believed a man to be the creator of all things. She was told that they were taking the children away from their families, forcing them to believe their ways. Some never to return home. These people, she was warned, were not like them; they were from another part of the world, they spoke a strange language, wore all black, tied long ropes around their waists and had shining crosses hanging from their necks.

Kǫ̀'s mother could see now that the warnings were true, but it was too late to take Kǫ̀ and run. Besides, she hadn't the strength. She was too weak with nausea and fatigue and knew they wouldn't make it very far even if they tried.

Like a swift summer sandstorm, the missionaries blew through the small communities that dotted the shoreline of the peninsula, silencing the children's laughter.

It was early spring and there were still heaps of heavy slush in the shadows and on the trails. The warmth of Kǫ̀'s mother's breath evaporated in the air in front of her when she bravely put on her shawl and stepped outside. She watched in shock as the burly men in red suits and black boots beat the mothers and fathers with long thick batons to keep them back when they tried to stop them from taking their children.

Kǫ̀ tried to see what was going on as he peeked out from behind his mother, who had stepped in front of him to block his view. She put her hand over his eyes as they approached Keeweetin's home but Kǫ̀ could see through the cracks in her fingers.

Although Keeweetin was fast and fit, the men in red suits outnumbered him. They chased him down and scooped him up by the stomach before he could get away. The men hung onto both his arms tightly as a man in black held a large wooden cross out in front of him, repeating a chant as he hovered his hand over Keeweetin's forehead. This only served to anger Keeweetin even more. He kicked and punched at the cloaked stranger who stood in front of him in patriarchy, his large black cloak churning in the changing winds.

Kǫ̀ mother gripped his hand tightly and met him at eye level. "Natǫmǫ̀eda-le," she whispered, telling him not to run or fight back.

"Nànetso xè netà wedanąą̀ɂı," she cried, telling him that he must be brave and wait for his father to bring him back home. She cleaned some of the noticeable dirt off his face with her thumb and smoothed down his hair. Then she kissed him on the forehead before walking out in front of him into the blinding sunshine.

With her head held high, she walked straight towards the fast-approaching boats, their oars ripping manically through the water, breaking through the last of the thin ice on the shoreline, cracking it like pieces of delicate glass.

The man with the cross stood up in the rocking canoe before it came to a sudden halt in front of their home. He waited for the Mounties to dock the boat on the smooth slippery rock and was helped out while the children inside the boat whimpered below him — except for Keeweetin, the only one in the boat not crying, his face as red as the blood of his last kill, a deeper shade than the red suits before him.

Kǫ̀ noticed right away how sickly the foreigner looked. He was pale and hunched over, and the sight of him up close must have made his mother ill, so much so that she couldn't hold in her overwhelming nausea. She tried to cover her mouth but it was no use. She heaved and heaved until she brought up the berries she ate that morning and quickly wiped her mouth clean with the back of her hand, brushing her tears away with her shawl. Kǫ̀ tried to help her by patting her back and holding her hair away from her face, but the men in red barged towards them with a blatant look of disregard, pushing past her and knocking her to the ground, looking down on her with disgust and leaving her to watch helplessly as they took her only child.

She got back to her feet quickly, not wanting Kǫ̀ to worry about her. With her hand on her stomach, she forced a smile at Kǫ̀, gently nodding at him to make sure he knew he was going to be okay, that she would be okay. Kǫ̀ trusted wholeheartedly that, upon his return, his father would band together with the other men in the community and bring the children back home from wherever they were going. He quietly got into the boat and found a spot to sit at the feet of the women in black, who sat motionless in the long canoe next to the captive children. Their hair was covered tightly in black cloth, the only part of their costume not flailing in the wind.

With the help of the men in red, the wretched man with the cross collected the rest of the children out of every home. One by one they were pushed into the large canoe until there was room for no more. As they turned away from the peninsula, Keeweetin, being the strong swimmer that he was, built up the courage to try to jump out of the boat but was pulled back in and shoved down. The men had no patience for Keeweetin's relentless determination, and Kǫ̀ saw the man in black give a nod to the larger of the men in red, the enforcer, giving him the go-ahead to apply more force. The man punched the boy hard on his temple, knocking him out cold.

Keeweetin was left lying at the bottom of the boat — a solemn reminder for the rest of the children to behave the rest of the way to a new land they had never seen.

Kǫ̀ tried to help his cousin, but he was hit hard across the hand with a strap by one of the disapproving women. With a mix of helplessness and anger, Kǫ̀ set his eyes out at the lake behind him, trying desperately to remember his way home. It was the first time he learned to numb his feelings. Little did he know that when they arrived at their destination, Keweetin would be unable to wake up. He would later be buried behind the schoolyard in one of many unmarked graves.

With his eyes wide, Kǫ̀ never blinked once as he mapped the route in his mind so that he would know where they were going and more importantly, so he would know his way back home.

That very day, Kǫ̀'s father was on his way home earlier than expected after a successful muskrat harvest. His dog team raced through the trails but when he heard the distant cries through the trees in the small communities that he passed on his way, he slowed down to be sure of what he was hearing.

Through the clearings, he saw weeping parents huddled at the shorelines. The sound of infants, too young to be taken away to school, mirrored the painful sobs in the sorrowful arms of their mothers.

Kǫ̀'s father sent his dogs into a fury as he lashed his whip on the ground next to them. Sounding off the alarm of the copper bells tied to the end of his whip, the sound rang louder than ever before as he headed towards home, hoping that he wasn't too late to save his son.

Summer passed by in a daze for Kǫ̀. He knew that winter was near because the school had become colder than usual. Children were falling ill with fever and blankets were scarce. A constant cough spread throughout the school and many children were too weak to do their daily chores but, in that place, there was no rest for the weary.

Kǫ̀ took it upon himself to do more than his share of work and did the chores for the younger children as often as he could. He got to know every creak in the floorboards, every corridor and every secret room where the cries of children could be heard behind closed doors. He did most of his work in the morning and was done his share by the time lunch was served so that he could do the work of others into the evening. Before dark he would chop wood outside of the school, saving the task of cutting wood for last. The fresh air and familiar chore were all that helped ease his longing for home.

Each quarter of the school had a nun designated to keep the children in order, and he learned that the nun watching over him was especially wicked above all the others for he had felt her wrath regularly and he steered clear of her as much as possible.

Every day after lunch, instead of going into the schoolyard with the other children, he would sit under the barred-up window at the end of the hallway. He'd long lost the desire to play outside confined behind a fence and would rather sit inside above it all, trying to see beyond the jail he was in. Barely able to bring his chin over the ledge, he would reach out his neck and look out from the grim grey school. There he would search beyond the empty brown field of the schoolyard for any sign of freedom.

Kǫ̀ couldn't keep count of the days, but he knew he had been there for some time through the slow passing of the seasons. After a while, he began to envision his father, armed with his skinning knife, walking towards the school in vigilance, ready to drive his blade into anyone who tried to stop him from bringing his son home.

He could see him clearly breaking trail through the trees that hovered above the tall wooden fence and through the brick walls that locked the children in and their families out. But it was mere hallucinations for nothing ever moved through the trees except the wind. Even though he knew that what his mind created wasn't real, it was difficult for Kǫ̀ to turn his gaze away from what was beyond the fence. Kǫ̀'s father was more of a ghost to him now; even so, he was a ghost that he did not ever want to lose sight of.

Along with learning the basics of English like handwriting his English name, Kǫ̀ and the other children were brought to a church on the grounds of the school every Sunday. They were taught to pray to a different god than the one he knew, a human god, but Kǫ̀ knew outright that his god was not human, and his god could not be found in a book. The land was his god, and it was more powerful above all else; his steadfast belief in Creator was all he had left to help him to get through the days.

Kǫ̀ remained strong in his spirituality even if it meant he would be punished for it. He stubbornly refused to pray to a statue, and the more he denied it the more he was made to repent. In his heart, though, he recounted his love for the land, the water, the animals and the sound of the drum that he could now only hear in his chest when he was afraid.

He knew their god could not save them if they were ever caught in a storm out on the land, not the way that his god had saved him in the form of an animal when he was lost on the trail in the storm. He would give anything to go back to that day, to be out in the tundra fighting for his life, than to have his dignity torn from him day after day in the prison he found himself locked in.

CHAPTER 4

It was in the residential school that Kǫ̀ first met Ts'ı. She stood quietly in line behind him on the first day there, shaking from cold or fear, or both, Kǫ̀ couldn't be sure. As soon as he heard her say her name, he knew it meant tree. Her name reminded him of the time he and his father camped out on the banks of a small lake they had to portage to, having crossed over the big lake and down the fast-moving river.

After hearing talks of something his father called the "Treaties," he'd brought Kǫ̀ along with him further south to see what was taking place. From the outskirts, they both watched the gatherings that were taking place at one of the forts. They weren't the only ones who had made the trip; there were many other witnesses present as the white men traded weapons for pelts with headmen from different communities. Kǫ̀ was still very young at the time, almost too young to remember, but he especially recalled the long trek further south for every so often he felt like asking how long it would be until they reached their destination, but he knew better than to aggravate his father with his needless requests.

They'd gone quite a distance to get a closer look at what was happening with the new type of trading between his people and the prospectors who were branching out further north for exploration. The journey would have taken them a few days by boat, but it took them a lot longer because Kǫ̀'s father made it a point to take a detour where they stopped and camped in a sheltered bay.

Kǫ̀'s father told him that the people that lived in that area spoke a language slightly different from their own, but if you listened closely, you could understand it. He told him they were visiting a sacred place, a place where a special tree grew.

"Jǫ t'a ts'ıhdeè neè hǫt'e," his father said. "Jǫ sìı got'aàʔà hǫt'e."

But Kǫ̀ was too distracted to listen to his father's teachings when he saw a large flock of seagulls lift into the sky in front of them in a startled flight after being disrupted from their nesting. The distraught birds hovered above Kǫ̀ and his father and flapped their wings, squawking wildly before nose-diving at the two floating figures. It was a warning to keep away from their nesting grounds where their eggs were hidden in the low brush that covered a small island, the open rock edges of it painted white.

Kǫ̀ had never seen a seagull before; his dad would later teach him that their summer migration patterns stopped short of going any further north. He feared the large angry white birds, their red bottom beaks blazing and he flailed his paddle in the air back and forth trying to protect himself. When all else failed, he ducked and covered his head with his arms but his only defence served to make things worse, as the birds took it upon themselves to splat all over him.

When they were finally in the clear, Kǫ̀ looked at his father dumbfounded. His father tried not to laugh, but he couldn't help himself and soon gave in to a burst of laughter as tears streamed down his face.

"Wet'à gots'ǫ̀xǫ̀ıdı."

His father told him it was a sign of good luck to lessen the embarrassment.

"Mbehk'ò." They're seagulls, he explained.

When they got closer to shore, Kǫ̀ dived off the boat to clean himself off. He swam to shore to meet up with his father; it was tough trying to find his footing as the land was sheathed in one big smooth, flat rock where a large spruce tree proudly grew right up and out of a crack that somehow pierced through the tough coat of armour standing the test of time.

The tree stood taller than all the other trees that Kǫ̀ had ever laid eyes on. His father explained, "Dìı ts'ıh sìı wezhǫ̀a xè naàtso," telling him that the powerful tree had been there for thousands of years and that because it was so strong, growing out of solid rock, it would not fall for another thousand years and when it did it would be a time of change. Kǫ̀ looked up at the mighty tree admiring its unique beauty.

"Ts'ı egeèda hǫt'e." His father picked up an acorn that fell from the large tree and held it in the palm of his hand. He gave the acorn to Kǫ̀ and told him that trees live and breathe just like humans and that it only takes one small acorn to grow an entire family of them.

Kǫ̀ remembered his father's words when he saw Ts'ı sitting alone outside in the schoolyard, crying after they had been at the school for more than a summer. He was in his usual spot, looking out the window hoping to see his father, when he saw her. She was turning over a small sprig of alder that had fallen into her lap from an overhanging branch that danced in the wind on the other side of the fence.

Wanting to help lift her out of her loneliness somehow, Kǫ̀ decided right then and there that the next day he would jump the fence and pluck one of the tiny budding green acorns from the tree to give to her so that maybe she could plant it in the ground and get her family back.

The next day, Kǫ̀ bravely walked to the edge of the fence careful not to move too quickly. Not wanting to bring attention to himself, he didn't dare look over at the nun on yard duty to see if she was watching him. Too afraid that the feeling of his eyes looking over at her would catch her attention, he kicked his feet at the dirt as he walked and kept his hands in his pockets.

It was a windy day, so much so that one of the alder trees was bent forward in the wind and over the fence making it look like it was bowing to an audience. As he got closer to the fence and his false sense of freedom, the wind rushed through the trees starting at the very end of the fence and continuing in a ghostly arrangement until reaching the tree that Kǫ̀ stood under, giving him just enough room to jump up and grab a clump of leaves. But instead, he ripped a whole branch off, a branch that held a cluster of small sticky ripe acorns nestled firmly into the twigs coming off the thick fresh brush. He hurriedly plucked just one and buried it deep down in his pocket and threw the branch back over the fence just before the children were rounded up to go inside for lunch.

"Did you know that acorns are seeds?" he said to Ts'ı as he walked up to her the next day in the schoolyard, once again leaving his post by the window, this time to join her at the same spot where she had been sitting alone the day before.

Ts'ı didn't look up. Even when he stood in front of her and blocked the sun, she still didn't look up at him. Instead, she looked through him blankly staring towards the steps leading up to the front doors of the school.

The nuns were on the move, which meant it was almost time to go back in and he was running out of time. He tried again. "I got this for you," he said as he dug into his pocket and pulled out the small broken acorn. It had crumbled apart in his pocket from being dried out and tossed around. Ts'ı stopped staring off into space and for a moment looked at what he held in his hand. Her eyes gave off a glimpse of sparkle when she saw that he was being kind. He took a chance and sat down beside her. She held her hand out but quickly closed it again when she saw the nun rushing towards them and they both jumped to their feet with looks of guilt.

"What's going on here? Boys and girls are not allowed to speak to each other. What did he give you? Open your hand right now!" the nun yelled before either of them could respond. She grabbed Ts'ı's wrist and hit her tightly closed fist with a black rubber strap, causing her dry knuckles to break open and bleed. Ts'ı crumpled her chin and opened her empty hand trying not to look at Kǫ̀. The nun turned to Kǫ̀, but before she could grab his hand, he popped half of the broken acorn in his mouth and swallowed it down in one hard gulp.

Ts'ı stared at Kǫ̀, her eyes wide in fear of what they would do to him for being so defiant. The nun let go of Ts'ı but not before she brutally whacked her on the side of the neck with her thick strap. Then nun grabbed Kǫ̀ roughly by his arm and dragged him up the school steps. He didn't struggle; instead, he let every muscle in his body loosen to make it harder for her to haul him. Even though he would have easily been able to take her down, he knew it would just make things worse for himself if he fought back so he surrendered to whatever punishment was coming his way but not before turning to look back at Ts'ı. He smiled at her apologetically as she held her neck, her mouth flat, but Kǫ̀ could see that she still had a small flicker of light in her eyes.

Ts'ı kept on the lookout for Kǫ̀ after that, but it would be a few days before he would be let out of confinement, a place that many children never returned from.

Once free, Kǫ̀ waited several days before he bravely snuck over to the girls' side of the schoolyard again when the nun on duty had turned the corner of the school and out of sight. The bruise on Ts'ı's neck from where the nun strapped her had, by then, turned a swampy green.

"Are you okay?" she asked when she saw him.

"Yeah," he said and patted his stomach then pointed to the biggest tree on the other side of the fence. "I'm going to grow strong like that tree and get us out of here."

Ts'ı chuckled, and her own laughter surprised her. She had often wondered the same thing he did — if happiness still existed.

Ts'ı's name had been changed to Therese by the nuns on her first day at the school, and even though she would nearly forget her true name over time, Kǫ̀ would remember it for her.

The image he had of her, scared and alone as she stood behind him in line, would never leave him for as long as he lived, and he knew he had to be strong, if not for himself, then for her. It was the caring for someone else that helped lift him out of his own unhappiness, if only for a time.

Kǫ̀ and Ts'ı would eventually forget their language altogether while at the school. Kǫ̀ spent one too many long winters in residence, never once allowed to leave, not even to go home for the summers like some children and neither was Ts'ı, which brought them even closer together.

The winter that he had been lost out in the tundra alone, starving and afraid to die, was nothing compared to what he experienced inside the walls of the school. His mind would go back to that time when he was out on the land alone, having to prove that he could survive. He would give anything to be free. To be where he felt that he belonged to something much bigger than himself. Being on the land was a different kind of vulnerability, it was the only place he felt alive.

Kǫ̀ took a rest from scrubbing the floor and looked out to see Ts'ı walking alone alongside the old rickety wooden fence that once towered over the schoolyard threateningly. The backdrop to their restricted lives had no real power to hold them in other than being a deterrent to running away.

It was a special day. It was the day that Ts'ı was allowed to leave. As carelessly as she was torn from her family, she would be tossed back into a world that she no longer knew. Now that it was assumed that Ts'i had aged out of the school system, she didn't know where she belonged.. She confided in Kǫ̀ that much of the memories of her family had been erased. She was ashamed that she no longer knew her family name or where she came from. She knew she wouldn't be returning to her family since the mission did a poor job of keeping records of where the children were from, and they had arranged for her to move to a small mining town where she would stay with a restaurant owner and work to pay for her room and board.

When he saw a black town car pull up to the school, Kǫ̀ ran to say goodbye. The nuns had become lenient over the years and stopped trying to keep the boys and girls from speaking to each other when out in the yard, not out of any kindness but of apathy.

Kǫ̀ was happy that she was finally getting out but sad at the same time because he couldn't go with her. All he knew for sure was that he was going to miss her the same way he missed his family. He clenched his jaw and forced a smile to prevent his upper lip from trembling.

Ts'ı saw him harshly wiping his tears away and gave him a long hug.

"I'm scared," she whispered.

"You're finally getting out of here."

He opened his hand and held out a small fresh green acorn to give to her.

"Remember me, okay."

"Of course," she started to laugh-cry, remembering the day he ate the acorn.

Kǫ̀ broke the acorn in half and gave her the top piece.

"Here. Take half. That way we'll always be together."

She held the acorn to her chest. "Goodbye Christian."

"Kǫ̀," he said.

Ts'ı looked confused.

"My real name's Kǫ̀," he answered.

She smiled. "Goodbye Kǫ̀," and gave him one last hug before walking slowly over to the waiting town car — unsure of her future and what awaited her beyond the fence.

Kǫ̀ gripped the acorn tightly at his side until his hand turned white. Ts'ı looked back one last time and, seeing Kǫ̀ as sad as he was, tossed the acorn in her mouth and swallowed it down hard before getting into the car.

"Now I'm strong like the tree, too," she said with a smile.

CHAPTER 5

When Kǫ̀ was finally allowed to go home, he didn't know where he was at first. He stepped off the tiny floatplane in a place the pilot referred to as Coppertown. He carried with him no luggage, not like the other passengers who had so much luggage he was afraid it would be too heavy for the plane to carry. All that Kǫ̀ had were the clothes on his back and the half-dried acorn in his pants pocket.

When he was forced to leave his home on the peninsula all those years ago, he didn't remember ever seeing a town. All he knew was that he summered in a small community surrounded by water as far as the eye could see.

When he got off the small plane at the dock in the old town, he was in the midst of a new and bustling mining town, a stranger on his own territory. Lost and turned around, Kǫ̀ didn't know which direction to go to head for home but soon recognized familiar landmarks when he looked past the muddy roads full of potholes haphazardly filled with rocks to keep cars from sinking into the deep trenches. Banks, restaurants and trading posts stood two stories high across from private docks reserved for twin otters and steamboats.

Kǫ̀'s feet were unsteady as he walked down the hill towards the place he remembered his home to be. When he arrived at the shack at the edge of the water, he was relieved to see the house which looked a lot smaller than he remembered. Over the years, the earth had begun taking it back, sinking it slowly with the constant flow of groundwater.

He straightened his collar and cleared his throat before knocking softly on the door, unsure if he should walk right on in. For a moment he doubted if anyone even lived there at all anymore after waiting for what seemed like an eternity.

He looked around to see any signs that the home was still occupied. The outside of the house was overgrown with tall weeds. Abandoned spider webs filled the empty spaces in the shadows. He knocked again, this time with more urgency, on the solid wooden door his father built. The same door that protected him from the howling winds so long ago.

He rubbed his neck with the stressful thought of the house being empty. Little did he know that his mother was inside and elbow deep in a big bowl of flour and water, mixing the ingredients with her hands to form palm-sized round pieces of what Kǫ̀ later learned was called bannock, a bread that transpired out of the establishment of the trading posts. She had been commissioned to make it for the local restaurant, one of the only ways she was able to get by.

She took her time collecting herself. If it were urgent they wouldn't have knocked so quietly, she thought, and she wasn't expecting any visitors The only visitors she ever got were expectant fathers coming to tell her that a baby was on the way, and they made no attempt at knocking; they just barged on in frantically, especially the first-time fathers.

She washed her hands in a basin of warm water, clouding it up, and wiped them dry on her apron before opening the door. When she first saw him she stepped back, unsure. She held her hand up over her eyes to block the sunlight streaming in from behind his silhouette and took a long look before falling into him and resting her head on his chest. He was so much taller than her now. She hugged him for a long time thankful that he was still alive and he didn't know to hug her in return but could feel how fragile she was. The young, strong, beautiful mother he held in his memory was now weary-eyed and frail.

The bright daylight shone in through the cracks between the moss in the walls as Kǫ̀ ducked his head to get in through the door.

He tried to speak in his first language to ask where his father was, but he wasn't able to string even the slightest bit of words together to form a sentence. He thought he could utter the words but they were trapped inside and wouldn't cut loose. When he did speak, he fumbled over and over again until giving up altogether.

There was so much left unsaid but how would he ever find the words to say what he needed to say.

She could see that he was distraught and reached up to put her hand on his shoulder, but he flinched and shielded himself with his forearm in defence, a reflex ingrained in him to protect himself from the blows at the mission. As soon is it happened, he wanted to apologize but couldn't.

"It's okay," she said. He was surprised she knew English and his deep brown eyes lit up.

"You speak English?"

"Some."

Even though they could converse in one word sentences, they said little to one another; both not knowing where to begin. Although the wedge between their bond was now removed it would still take time to begin where they left off.

Kǫ̀ waited until she fell asleep to go for a walk. He tried to quietly shut the door but it creaked loudly as he walked out of the small unfamiliar home and up the hill, through the streets of the town that destroyed the pristine untouched lands he knew so well. It left him with the sense that he no longer knew where he belonged; he was now a stranger on his own land. Even more, he still did not know where his father was now that he was home.

He needed answers but at the same time, he was afraid to ask. Afraid to know. The slight language barrier between Kǫ̀ and his mother was the only thing keeping him from knowing what happened to his father; in a way, he was okay with it, for he wasn't sure he was ready to know the truth.

CHAPTER 6

Over the years, Kǫ̀ and his mother would make small breakthroughs in communicating with each other. Kǫ̀ helped her to improve her English and she helped him to relearn his first language all over again. He winced when the words came out, but he was eventually able to form fragmented sentences that his mother could understand.

When Kǫ̀ could finally string enough words together to ask his mother what happened to his father, he still couldn't bring himself to ask her for fear of what the the answer might be.

Questions about his father did not get in the way of him wanting to rebuild the severed bond with his mother. He saw that the house required a lot of work to keep it from caving in on itself, and even though he didn't know what it was to be a son, he knew he needed to at least be useful and so he went to work repairing the house for her.

Having Kǫ̀ around gave his mother a break from the monotonous duties of the self-sustaining life she lived. She was able to get back to the things she loved and began making clothing for Kǫ̀ that would keep him warm in the coming winter.

At the mission, Kǫ̀ often reminisced about being back out on the land and how everything would go back to the way it was once he returned home, but now that he was home he still felt the same sinking loneliness he had felt at the school. Even with the land outside his doorstep, Kǫ̀ couldn't find freedom. Partly because he didn't have the means to travel very far without a boat or a dog team.

Kǫ̀'s mother could sense he had a longing, that something was missing in his life. She often caught him staring out at the lake in quiet thought and wanted to help but didn't know how. Then she remembered the one thing that his father left behind, that wasn't destroyed by the Mounties.

She met Kǫ̀ outside that very evening in the restless winds. His day was nearly done when she came up to him and rested her hand on his shoulder. He had just finished piling enough wood to last them the rest of the winter and had propped up the woodpile against one side of the house to help keep it from collapsing. "Jǫ̀ıtł'e," she said, and he wiped the sweat off his forehead and followed her. She led him to a grassy bank behind the house where the wind blew stronger off the lake, tossing the tall grass wildly in all directions.

She lifted a row of heavy rocks that were fixed atop a dry pile of long yellow grass and started tearing away at the shreds. Kǫ̀ helped her, not knowing what she was up to until he saw it. His father's old canoe turned upside down and hidden from sight.

It was the very same boat he sat in many times with his father as they pulled in their fishing nets. In the spring, they filled it to the brim with rows of geese, so much so that the water would meet the level of the boat and spill inside, and it was Kǫ̀'s job to bail it out. He would spend days upon days plucking and singeing the geese. At the sight of the canoe, he was brought right back to the better part of his childhood again, if only for an instant. As he glided his hand across the bottom of the smooth, waxed birch bark, his mother was pleased that she was able to put a smile on his face.

He would have to wait until most of the ice melted to put it in the water but already the excitement of being back out on the water was replaced with a deep sense of fear. A fear that he might have forgotten all that he was taught. Still, his desire to be out on the water outweighed his panic and he made up his mind that he would head out as soon as the weather would allow it.

Kǫ̀ busied himself repairing the boat, checking for holes, packing, unpacking and packing again until he was sure he could fit everything he needed. When the time came, he lifted the canoe over his head with ease and made his way down to the lake behind his house.

He was still somewhat hesitant; in fact, he may not have even gone if the sun weren't shining, if the water wasn't sparkling the way it did, inviting him with its brilliance. It was a perfect day, and he found no excuse to not go. The moment he dipped his paddle into the ice-cold water, life made sense again and he felt as calm as the lake before him.

He made his way steadily until he reached the mouth of the river and made a sharp turn, putting his hand into the frigid water every so often and wiping the sweat off his face as the sun beat down on him. Halfway down the river, a small red fox jumped between the reeds along the shoreline, searching for mice. He felt a set of watchful eyes on him and looked up to see an old bald eagle looking down from a tall tree, its nest hanging over a rocky cliff. The eagle he had carved as a child, once unfinished, come to life. A beaver dived under the water and splashed his tail at Kǫ̀, angry that he had interrupted his busy task of fixing up his home. Kǫ̀ laughed at himself when he realized that the splash of the beaver's tail had startled him, and his laughter bounced off the cliffs that surrounded the riverbend. The echo took him by surprise, and he laughed even more. Purposefully. Nearly crazed. It was the first time he had laughed since he could remember. Then his laugh turned into a yell. Alone with his thoughts, safe from judgment, where no one could hurt him.

Even though he had changed, the land had stayed the same. After all that time, it hadn't let him down and, in that revelation, Kǫ̀ found solace.

Before he knew it, Kǫ̀ found himself headed towards a special place. He allowed the pull of the river to guide him to where his heart needed to go. He camped that night in a small bay near the rapids. This would not be a trip to harvest; he would save that for his next journey. For now, he needed to explore.

He kept onwards until he banked his canoe and bushwhacked his way through overgrown trail in search of the place where he and his father had portaged at a time that now seemed like a lifetime ago. The first thing Kǫ̀ spotted when he returned to the rock where the sacred tree stood were the seagulls and Kǫ̀ steered hard in the opposite direction to give their nesting place a wide birth, not wanting to disturb the overly protective flock.

Looking up at the tall tree instantly brought thoughts of Ts'ı to Kǫ̀'s mind. He had often found himself missing her. He wanted nothing more now than to see her again, his only friend, and wondered if he would ever have the chance.

He said a silent prayer for Ts'ı and wished her well. It was the first time in a long time that he had prayed to the God that he knew. He knelt under the sacred tree, picked up a small acorn, gripping it tightly in his hand and closed his eyes. It was there that he was finally able to begin to let go of all that was lost and might never be found.

On his return home, Kǫ̀ took the long way around. He returned to the waterfall where he once sat next to his father on their last hunting trip together. As he floated on the rocky shoreline downstream of the waters that once seemed larger than life itself, he saw a large white object in the shallows at the far end of the bay. He paddled towards it but got stuck in the horsetail reeds that as a child he pulled apart and put back together like a puzzle. He jumped from the canoe and waded in the water towing the boat behind with a rope until he saw that it was a muskox skull lying sideways in the clear water.

He held it by one of its horns and turned it over to find dozens of flies come flying through its hollowed eye sockets and stepped back. He washed his hands in the water knowing it could only mean one thing.

He looked up at the mouth of the waterfall half expecting to see the picture his father had painted in his mind so long ago of the muskox and the bison, but there was nothing except the sight and sound of the waterfall crashing down in front of him, hitting him with the sense that the world had become off balance since he had been there last.

Kǫ̀ was never home for long. He would come home only to bring his mother whatever he had caught in his fishing nets or traplines and would set out again after a day or two of visiting. Being out on the land was the only thing that made him forget.

As time passed, Kǫ̀ began to accept that it was just him and his mother and that he might never know what happened to his father.

Then, one evening, as Kǫ̀ pulled his canoe to shore behind the house after a good day out on the water, he saw a young man who looked familiar, almost like looking at his own reflection, so much so that he couldn't help but stop and stare.

"I've been told that I might find my mother in this area," said the young man. His hand shook as he held out a piece of crumpled up paper to show to Kǫ̀.

"I … don't remember her name but I might know her if I see her," he said hopefully.

Kǫ̀ looked puzzled. "Who are you?" He stepped closer trying to get a better look at the boy.

The young man pointed at his papers now in Kǫ̀'s hand.

"My name's Woods. It's short for Woodrow. I ... I don't know my Indian name," he stumbled.

The longer that Kǫ̀ looked at the boy, the more he saw the distinct traits of his father. The bulky build, the deep distinctive voice. The only difference Kǫ̀ could see between the kid in front of him and his father was the age difference and the way he wore his hair. Instead of one long braid, the kid sported dark thick, fluffy hair that looked like it had grown out from a uniform bowl cut to being curled out behind his ears.

Kǫ̀'s mother heard Kǫ̀ talking to someone and came out of the house to see who it was. When she looked up to see Woods, she reached out for him with open arms. "Nene," she cried and put her hands to her mouth unable to believe what she was seeing. Her happiness was so overwhelming that she had to go inside and sit down with the help of both men at her side, the two estranged brothers looking at one another in confusion.

"He has no father," the nuns told Kǫ̀'s mother as she tried to hold onto the last of her family.

"He needs to learn to read and write," they said.

His mother couldn't understand the harsh words that were spoken as the nuns ripped her youngest from her grip. Nene was too small to be taken, still a baby, but that didn't matter to the nuns.

Kǫ̀ tried to piece it all together. He searched his memory for any sign of a brother, and it was then that he was suddenly struck with the recollection of the day he stepped onto the boat when the missionaries came to take him away.

The ice had just melted over the lake, and only shattered pieces of dark black glass hugged the shoreline. Kǫ̀ turned to look one last time at his mother. She was pale and bent over holding her large expectant belly. He was about to be a big brother. He closed his eyes hard and tried to remember more. He started to recall the smells but all he could take in was the strong smell of sweat coming off the priest's dirty robe. Then he started to remember the sounds.

Over the sound of water splashing violently he heard them. The sound of bells — the sound of copper bells tied to a dog team growing louder and faster as they raced towards him, but the sound of the paddles next to Kǫ̀'s head breaking through the still water rowed faster and further away eventually drowning out the last sounds he would ever hear of his father.

CHAPTER 7

When the settlers tried to trade with Kǫ̀, he turned them down every time. He had no use for their fancy things. Flour, sugar, tobacco, moonshine and guns were the most popular commodities, but Kǫ̀ did not trust their offerings, nor did he have any use for them.

Whenever he agreed to make the trip to town for his mother he ducked in and out quickly, trying to remain unnoticed. Every day, the prospectors were out on the docks measuring piled furs to the length of the barrel of a gun for trade. But Kǫ̀ had no use for their guns. He didn't think it right to exploit animals — killing them for nothing other than their skins and tossing the meat to scavengers, messing up the natural order of things.

The day Kǫ̀'s mother heard that a supply of colourful glass beads had come off one of the floatplanes she asked Kǫ̀ to make the trip to town before they were all gone, and even though he could think of a million other things he'd rather do, he went because he knew how important it was to her. He almost felt bad for not wanting to go as she had been saving up the money she made from selling her bannock for the day the beads arrived. Little did he know she was planning on surprising him with a fancy beaded vest, one for Kǫ̀ and one for Nene, both matching. The kind with a fringe like she had seen other people in the community wearing on special occasions.

As Kǫ̀ walked into town, he kept an eye out for Woods. The last time he saw him at the house some of their mother's money had gone missing. Kǫ̀ confronted Woods but their mother stood in the way, not wanting an argument between her two boys, "Hot'a. Esąnìle."

Kǫ̀ soon learned that he couldn't rely on Woods to help him to take care of their mother for the simple fact that when he said he was going to do something he would rarely show up.

Nevertheless, Woods moved in and lived with Kǫ̀ and their mother at first, but his drinking was out of control from the start. On more than one occasion, Woods would come home well into the night, slurring, and trying to start fights while Kǫ̀ was fast asleep. Many times, Kǫ̀ had to defend himself; luckily, he was the stronger of the two. The fight would end with both of them on the floor, Kǫ̀ on top holding him down and threatening to punch him if he kept it up, only to get off him when their mother woke and begged for the fighting to stop.

Woods eventually moved out on his own without Kǫ̀ having to tell him to leave. He didn't announce that he was leaving, he just slowly transitioned into living a wandering lifestyle. Kǫ̀ knew where he could be found. He often saw Woods hanging outside the local bar on the streets of Coppertown. His mother's errands had turned into a way of keeping an eye on Woods.

Since establishments didn't serve alcohol to anyone with dark skin it didn't take long for Woods to get involved in bootlegging to make his living while at the same time supporting his growing drinking problem.

Kǫ̀ walked through the narrow streets of town shortly after Woods left home for good. He could see the floatplane carrying his mother's precious beads coming in for a landing.

His feet moved quickly towards the dock. He wanted to get back to his fishing net before someone else came along and found his secret spot. As he walked past a small log house restaurant halfway up the hill to Coppertown, it was then, from the other side of the road, that he heard a familiar voice that made him stop in his tracks.

"Bobby, the garbage is piling up …"

Kộ strained his ear to listen hard.

"Can you take it out back, please?"

Her voice, like that of a songbird, was coming from behind the screen door at the back of the restaurant. Kộ followed the sound of the familiar voice and found himself at the top of the stairs listening carefully to be sure it was her. He put his hand up to peer in through the dark mesh screen to try and see inside, but just then, Bobby threw open the door with a bag full of trash in hand, knocking Kộ off the small stoop.

"Whoa, sorry mister. Are you okay?" the boy asked, trying to help Kộ up off the ground, but Kộ didn't need help and got back up on his feet before the boy could finish his sentence. He dusted himself off and made his way back onto the steps mere inches from Bobby's face and held his shoulders, shaking him out of excitement.

"Tell me there's a girl in there named Therese." Kộ desperately needed to know.

The boy seemed confused by Kộ's behaviour, but nodded his head yes. As if he could fly, Kộ jumped down all the steps and ran to the front door of the restaurant to greet her properly but he stopped short and thought about what he would say. Words alone were not enough. He needed to bring her something, a gift.

Without another thought, Kộ ran home and grabbed the bottom piece of the crumpled acorn he had been holding onto since he last saw her. It was where it always was, tucked safely away under his pillow, folded neatly into a piece of soft moose-hide. His mother looked at him questionably as he ran back out the door.

Forgetting all about his mother's beads, he ran all the way back to the restaurant without tiring. He burst excitedly into the small log cabin. People were sitting on rows of wooden benches with pieces of his mother's bannock in front of them on the table next to a small assortment of butter, syrup and jam. The patrons, only rich old white folks, looked up at him all at once, worried about his next move, but Kǫ̀ paid no mind and walked straight to the back of the kitchen where his old friend stood with her back to him washing dishes.

"Ts'ı."

"Ts'ı, it's me, Kǫ̀."

Ts'ı dropped the dish she was scrubbing into the large tub of water, where it sank to the bottom and broke. She turned around to face him, knowing it was him before he could say another word. He was the one and only person besides her family that knew her real name. Tears filled her eyes and she tried to wipe them away, but her hands were full of soap and all she could do was laugh and cry at the same time.

Kǫ̀ held out his hand and showed her the acorn. He shrugged one shoulder as he smiled shyly, feeling silly for thinking it might still mean something to her. Ts'ı smiled back and gave him a big bear hug. Bobby stood at the back of the kitchen, holding onto the mop awkwardly, and slowly started to whistle to politely break up their surprise reunion.

Suddenly embarrassed, Ts'ı broke their embrace and walked across the uneven wooden floor to the corner of the small kitchen and hung up her apron.

"Bobby, can you cover for me for a little while?"

She grabbed Kǫ̀ by the hand and walked away quickly before Bobby could answer.

The two long-lost friends walked side by side, crossing over dirt roads until they reached the edge of town where they sat on a rock cliff that towered over the slow-moving water below. With their feet dangling over the edge, they spent the afternoon catching up on each other's lives. It was where Kǫ̀ would sometimes go to admire the beauty of the river from above, near the eagle's nest made of both new and old brush nestled into the cracks high on a straight-drop cliff.

Kǫ̀ had so many questions to ask Ts'ı but didn't know where

to begin. Of all the places she could be, he wouldn't have guessed she'd been living in the same town as him all this time.

"You mean you were here all along?" he asked when she told him how long she'd been working at the restaurant.

Ts'ı nodded and laughed at his dumbfounded look, "I'm surprised I haven't run into you."

"Oh well I don't go into town much. Just to get a few things for ma here and there."

"Your mom? That's nice." Ts'ı looked down at her feet hanging over the rock cliff and suddenly became afraid of heights. She moved back a few inches and hugged her knees.

"It's just the two of us right now. Now that the weather's getting warm, I'm going to start fixing up the roof for her; it's been leaking. What about you? Are you back with your family?"

Ts'ı shook her head slowly. "I met some of my cousins. They told me my parents died not long after they took me away." She gulped mid-sentence. "They died from a sickness that they say spread like a wildfire. TB they call it."

"I'm sorry Ts'ı." Kǫ̀ couldn't help but wonder if what happened to T'si's parents might have been what happened to his father too, but he felt selfish at the same time turning to his own need for answers.

Ts'ı changed the subject, telling Kǫ̀ all about her job at the restaurant and what it was like having to live with the owners. That she worked to pay for her room and board and how the workers stayed up all night every night playing cards for money, making it hard for her to get any sleep. Her bed was tucked away in a small room in the back where smoke and drunken laughter drifted in.

"Come stay with me and my mom," he blurted but then realized it was probably too soon to ask her anything of the sort.

She smiled. "That's nice of you, Kǫ̀."

They talked until they both ran out of things to say, the two of them happy just to be in each other's presence. Kǫ̀ didn't doubt that it was more than chance that brought them together; it had to have been fate that their journeys led them to the same place, to that very moment in time. Kǫ̀ wanted to come right out and tell her how he felt about being able to see her and talk to her again. Just as he gathered up the courage, Ts'ı noticed the sun sinking fast behind a wall of pink clouds, and she got up in a rush, wiping the dirt off the back of her dress.

"It's getting late. I've got to get back to the restaurant. The time just got away..."

Kǫ̀ quickly got to his feet too, "I'll walk you back." But he could have just as well stayed sitting there with her forever.

Kǫ̀ visited Ts'ı every day after that. His shoes were soon worn out from making the long trek into town, but he didn't care. To be able to spend time with Ts'ı was more than he could ask for.

Kǫ̀ soon invited Ts'ı home, where his mother gave Ts'ı a big hug and instantly sized her feet for slippers, tracing the outlines of her bare feet onto a piece of soft tanned moose hide to be made into a pair of moccasins adorned with the glass beads that Kǫ̀ nearly forgot to pick up for his mother the day they reunited.

"So where are you taking me exactly?" Ts'ı asked Kǫ̀ as she stood in the summer sun watching him load supplies into the canoe.

"You'll see," he said. "It's a surprise."

Ts'ı frowned and looked to the side, "I'm not sure I like surprises."

"You're going to like this one, trust me," he said, smiling and looking up at her. The sun shining down on her dark brown hair made it look like it had bits of gold in it.

Ts'ı sat in the front of the canoe and paddled cautiously down the shallow river while Kǫ̀ sat in the back and steered.

They took their time, stopping along the way, but only for a few minutes as stopping to rest meant turning in circles with the steady current.

When they reached the bend where they could see the sacred tree standing tall above the rest, early childhood memories came flooding back to Ts'ı and she dropped her paddle in the water, leaving Kǫ̀ to have to reach for it as they floated by.

"I've been here!" she shouted excitedly and stood up in the canoe, nearly tipping it over.

"Easy," Kǫ̀ said, trying to steady the rocking boat. Ts'ı sat down quickly, but her hands were shaking .

"I know this place. This is home. I remember."

She closed her eyes to see better. "My grandfather. He named me," she said, now fighting back tears at the memory of him. Her mind went back to the day that he had brought her to the sacred tree. The day he told her the story of her family.

"He told me that the rock here was called Kwe." She could see clearly her grandfather kneeling to her level picking up a small rock, tossing it up in the air and catching it.

"Kwe," he said and knocked on it, telling her to look down and all around, pointing out the simple fact that they were surrounded by it. *"Dıı neè ı̨tà hazhǫ ı̨t'ǫ̀a hǫt'e ı̨lè."* He told her that the land flourished with flowers before the rock formed and that it had to do away with beauty, it had to harden itself to prepare for the coming of the changing winds. He told her that the land was once a very hot place a long time ago and that was why the sacred tree still stood strong, to remind people of the way things used to be. *"Degàe hǫt'e."* Which is why it is to be honoured for its strength and resilience, he explained wisely.

Ts'ı's grandfather told her that she was named after the tree and because of that she would carry with her both beauty and strength. That she would endure hardship and witness many changes in her lifetime yet remain strong through it all.

He told her that just by observing the tree and the way that it changed in each season one could learn everything there was to know about life.

Ts'ı opened her eyes and looked at Kǫ̀ curiously.

"How did you know about this place?"

"My father brought me here when I was young. He told me it was a special place. Now I know why it reminded me of you all this time."

"How can I miss what I've never really known?"

"Its your home. It's a part of you."

"I wouldn't have ever known the way back here. I would have never found home."

Kǫ̀ did his best to make the house accommodating for Ts'ı. He finished the repairs on the roof and added an addition out of the wood he harvested, stripped smooth and dried. It took him through late fall and right up until the first snowfall to complete, but when he was finished, the shack stood stronger than ever. The house already had a place to store and prepare food, a living area with a woodstove and a honey bucket out back, but it felt like home more than ever now that Ts'i was in it.

It was a very modest home. They didn't need much and because Kǫ̀ was able to provide for them through hunting and fishing Ts'ı was able to quit her job at the restaurant and begin helping Kǫ̀'s mother deliver babies instead. Kǫ̀'s mother had been delivering babies for the women on the peninsula whenever the doctor wasn't able to fly in in time. When she started bringing Ts'ı along to help with the births, Ts'ı's job was to mostly make sure there were enough towels, blankets and warm water on hand.

Word got around Coppertown that Kǫ̀'s mother was a midwife. When asked for help by one of the women up the hill she couldn't say no, and so she began helping the kwet'ı̨̀ı̨ bring their children into the world too, all the while never asking for anything in return.

Ts'ı learned that the women referred to Kǫ̀'s mother as a "midwife" while Kǫ̀ referred to his mother's role as dǫ ehda ayehʔı̨ hanı̀-le dè ts'eke hòtı̨ı̀ɂeda-le ts'adı̀ meaning life giver, which Ts'ı appreciated much more as it aligned with her own thoughts on the sacredness of giving birth. Having children of her own wasn't something Ts'ı had given much thought to. She wasn't sure she would know how to be a mother since the only child-rearing lessons she received were from the nuns, who had no patience for her. But being around Kǫ̀'s mother was healing for Ts'ı whether she knew it or not, and she naturally began calling her "Mamia" without even realizing it.

Under one roof, Kǫ̀, Ts'ı and Mamia lived a quiet life. Their home stood where it always did, at the end of the peninsula, in the same spot where Kǫ̀'s mother packed him on her back when he was a baby as she went about her day. In fact, she still had with her the cradle board that she made and carried her two sons in. It was a simple invention meant to hold babies in securely so that a mother's hands could be free to go about their work while at the same time it was a work of art. Its soft caribou hide and crisscrossed sinew overlayed across weaved willow sticks was pliable enough to bend yet strong enough to safely carry a delicate baby. Little did Ts'ı know that Mamia's old cradle board was soon to be dusted off and used again.

A new mother had come by the house in the dead of winter with her baby tucked under her jacket, shivering.

"Come," Mamia motioned her inside where Ts'ı quickly shut the door to keep the rush of cold air out.

The young woman was distraught. "I've been up all night with him. I don't know what to do. He won't stop crying." The woman bounced the baby and patted its bottom but the child just wailed and wailed. Mamia helped lift the baby out of her coat and wrapped him in a warm blanket that was hanging by the woodstove and handed him over to Ts'ı who patted the baby's back as his head bobbed on Ts'ı's shoulder. Ts'ı carefully sat down next to the woodstove looking unsure of herself as Kǫ̀ walked in the door from chopping wood to see what the visitor wanted. Normally, the two women in his life would be off in a hurry when someone came calling.

Mamia told Kǫ̀ to go back outside and continue working to give the woman her privacy. As Ts'ı steadied herself into a cross-legged position on the floor and moved the baby into a cradled position, she looked down at his steel-blue eyes and could see that he was trying to reach his hands into his mouth to suckle. She gently brushed his smooth head and soothed him with a light humming sound, and he slowly started to calm in her arms. Mamia was already preparing medicine for the mother, stirring a thick brew of dried leaves in the cast iron pot on the woodstove. "Here," she said and touched her own chest to show the woman that she needed to put it on her breast to help the milk to flow.

"But it hurts," the woman said and crossed her arms.

Mamia could see that one of the woman's breasts was larger than the other, swollen red and hot to the touch — a blocked duct wasn't allowing the milk to flow and the baby was hungry.

"Here." Mamia carefully placed the warm mixture onto her

skin with a piece of softened birch bark and the woman sighed with instant relief as the milk began to flow again.

Mamia motioned for her to feed her child but saw that the child was already fast asleep with his thumb in his mouth as Ts'ı continued to hum to him. Mamia gave the woman a small cup to pump her milk instead and use for later but the woman refused and pushed it back "No. No. He drinks from a bottle." Mamia looked confused.

"I don't feed him like that," the woman protested. Mamia had heard that some of the women from town did not nurse their babies and used cows' milk instead but she didn't believe it until then. Not one to judge, Mamia said no more and went about tidying.

"Thank you for your help," the woman said and started to put on her jacket to leave, nearly forgetting about her baby until Mamia reminded her. The woman walked over to Ts'ı and looked at her with an expression of fear that said she wasn't ready to be a mother. Ts'ı gently placed the baby back in his mother's arms trying not to wake him, but he was startled with the slightest movement and erupted into a full-blown scream. The woman looked at Mamia for answers, but she already knew what Mamia was going to say.

Mamia pointed with her chin to the spot where Ts'ı was sitting, and the woman hesitantly sat down by the fire with the same scared look in her eyes. Mamia draped the blanket over the young mother's shoulder, and the woman looked up at her with a look of shame as if what she was about to do was something forbidden, but her baby's cries grew more impatient and she could no longer hold off, his starvation imminent.

She put him to her breast, and for a moment he gurgled and choked under the flood of milk that flowed as if a dam had been broken but he didn't give up. The pair soon got the hang of it and when he seemed to have had enough, Mamia took him up in her arms and patted his back firmly. After a few raps, the infant belted out the loudest burp any of them had ever heard, and it was such an unexpected surprise out of the tiny baby that they all couldn't help but burst into laughter.

Mamia turned her attention to Ts'ı once their visitors had left and in her own quiet way, said "Hotìeɂeda-le." Ts'ı turned to Kǫ̀ who was now back in from the cold, his cheeks dotted white and his nose dripping with clear runny snot that he wiped off with the back of his sleeve. "What are you saying, Mamia?" he asked to be sure. Mamia rubbed her stomach and looked at Ts'ı. Ts'ı laughed nervously, "Oh no. Not yet. Not anytime soon." She looked at Kǫ̀, hoping his mother was teasing. Mamia just looked at her in her all-knowing way. "Baby told me," she said and sure enough Ts'ı and Kǫ̀ would be welcoming their baby into the world by the fall.

As their family grew, so did the world outside. Up the hill, Coppertown was rapidly expanding, overrun with competitors trying to stake land claims to dig for gold.

Large two-storey homes and rows of government office buildings were built at the top of the hill, along the pristine shoreline of the lake, the area that Kǫ̀ often heard referred to as "prime property." There was no mistaking that the settlers were there to stay. Still, Kǫ̀ stood strong in his dealings and was able to remain somewhat distanced from the townspeople. Despite the ever-present encroachment, Kǫ̀ and his family still lived off the land in every way possible, and in that way, it wasn't hard for him to hold off on having to rely on their contemporary ways of life.

The sun beamed down on Kǫ̀ most mornings when he walked out the front door, welcoming him to the beginning of each new day. Bright sun on a winter day meant it would be colder than usual but whatever the weather, it didn't faze him. He reveled in nature's discomfort. Being able to be outdoors doing what he loved, knowing that his loved ones were warm and safe was all that he needed in life. He ended his hard-working days under the moonlight that sparkled through the windowpane, giving off just enough light for Kǫ̀ to admire the reflection that bounced off T'si's golden-brown hair, matching her bright eyes.

For Ts'ı, living with Kǫ̀ and his mother was more than she could have asked for. Although living entirely off the land wasn't what she was used to, having grown accustomed to running water and electricity, she was happy. The love she felt radiating through her made her heart sing. She finally knew what it was like to have a family.

The three of them laughed under the light of the coal oil lamp each night as they told stories. Mamia liked to turn up the radio whenever one of Elvis's gospel songs came on and the baby seemed to like Elvis's voice because every time one of his songs played the baby kicked under Ts'ı's thin stretched belly. Kǫ̀ didn't care for Elvis's church music, but he let it go knowing Mamia enjoyed it. She had a soft spot for Elvis, once saying that he resembled his father when she first saw a picture of him in an ad in the black and white newspaper that her beads were wrapped in.

One evening, as they all sat together while Kǫ̀ was guessing whether it was an elbow or a foot poking out of Ts'ı's belly, they were interrupted by the sound of someone banging loudly on the door. It was the last person Kǫ̀ was expecting to see. "Kǫ̀, you gotta come see this," Woods said, taking a quick swig of moonshine from a clear glass jar.

"What is it?" Kǫ̀ asked, taking Woods half seriously as he had a sobering tone to his voice that Kǫ̀ could pick out through the slur.

"The settlers moved down the hill. Looks like they're here to stay," Woods said, swaying.

Kǫ̀ threw on his boots and grabbed his jacket and hat, pushing past Woods.

"Show me where."

Woods led the way, loudly singing one of Elvis's church hymns out of pitch, having caught the last bit of it playing on the radio, and Kǫ̀ followed, rolling his eyes.

Kǫ̀ hoped it wasn't true, that Woods was off on another one of his drunken tangents. But when they reached the marshy edge of the lake and saw a rickety barge with building supplies floating in the shallow waters somewhat hidden among the brush, he knew Woods was telling the truth. The settlers had set up camp on the peninsula and were already busy constructing roads and permanent structures in the area from what Kǫ̀ could see in the dark. He followed large tire tracks to a set of red tractors, their front wheels half stuck in the mud.

"We gotta stop 'em, Kǫ̀, they're gonna take over," Woods said clearly. "They're backing us into a corner." The cold blasts of air in his face on the walk had, by that point, sobered him up completely. He had long polished off his bottle of moonshine, having thrown the empty glass into the ditch and shattering the bottle, annoyed that he wasn't able to keep a steady buzz.

"How?" Kǫ̀ asked, more to himself than to his brother as he stared at the barge in front of them, his eyes unmoving, his mind stuck in deep thought.

"Chase 'em off," Woods said angrily, spit flying out of his mouth. He picked up a short stick and threw it pitifully at one of the tractors, losing his balance in the process.

"Go home and get some sleep. I'll talk to you in the morning," Kǫ̀ said, and he stood there alone in quiet thought as Woods staggered back home grumbling to himself.

Coppertown mocked Kǫ̀.

Invisible boundary lines were drawn out and mapped by the townspeople. No-go zones were put up. Big signs in red letters that Kǫ̀ couldn't read that said "K-e-e-p O-u-t" and "P-r-i-v-a-t-e P-r-o-p-e-r-t-y" were popping up everywhere Original prospectors named new roads either after themselves or the explorers that came before them, praising each other as trail-blazers, not taking into consideration that the people down the hill on the peninsula had their own trails. Trails that had been there all along, and their own names for the land at the top of the hill and under every rock.

The townspeople and the government gave themselves the go-ahead to expand further onto Kǫ̀'s homeland, leaving Kǫ̀ to worry that it was only a matter of time until his expansive hunting grounds would be mapped out and made off-limits. He wanted to stop them, needed to stop them, but didn't know how or where to begin. Besides, he couldn't go to war now; he was needed elsewhere. He was about to be a father.

CHAPTER 8

Their son was born on the same day the settlers were giving thanks by cooking turkeys in top-of-the-line convection ovens and dishing the golden-brown birds onto plates next to roasted vegetables that they grew in the dark imported soil neatly landscaped between the rock beds in their fenced-in backyards that Kộ observed on his walks into town.

On the day that the settlers set aside to be thankful, Kộ and Ts'ı were grateful too but not in the same way. The townspeople celebrated their own successes, raising their glasses in cheers to what they believed to be their triumph over the North, while Kộ and his family were thankful to have a healthy son born nearly the same size as one of the birds being carved at the dinner tables up the hill.

Kộ and Ts'ı were thankful on the day that their son came quietly into the world in a remarkably fast labour, but also grateful to Creator for blessing them with a healthy child every day after that too.

Kộ learned all about the practice of Thanksgiving by watching how the settlers prepared their feasts after slaughtering their shipped-in farm animals — pigs, cows, chickens and turkeys that came from the south only to be sold at the local trading post. Kộ didn't have to witness the dinner himself; he already knew that they would be sharing stories of land grabs over too much food, their bellies bloating with each mouthful.

Even if Kộ could have, he wouldn't have wanted that life. He was happy to be at home, thankful to share a meal with his family consisting of boiled caribou heart from a bull Kǫ̀ hunted the year before. He had saved the best parts of the caribou for when his firstborn was to arrive. Since the caribou were becoming noticeably scarce and moving further and further away each year, he was beginning to wonder when he might next be able to have a chance to see the migratory herd. The landscape seemed to be changing before his very eyes.

Kǫ̀ learned in residential school that the days were marked by the missionaries on what they referred to as a calendar. When Kǫ̀ first saw one, he found it strange to see each day numbered inside of a small box so when he saw one hanging on the wall at the trading post he scoffed. Like the clock on the wall behind the man, Kǫ̀ had no use or need to rely on a machine or a piece of paper to tell him the time of day or year. He knew the days and the time just fine without having to be told. It was found in the stars, in the changes in weather, the shift between night and day.

Their second child did not come into the world as easily. The baby had been in the breech position right up until it was time to deliver. Mamia tried to turn the baby early on, halfway through the pregnancy once she knew that the baby's round head was near Ts'ı's ribcage, but it was too painful for Ts'ı to endure the twisting and turning as Mamia tried to maneuver the baby around while Ts'ı lay flat on her back, groaning in pain.

Mamia had delivered thousands of babies by then and had seen breech positions before but with every breech she was able to help turn the baby's head down before labour. Yet, try as she might, there was no way the baby would budge. Mamia knew that the birth would be dangerous and tried every day to massage the baby into a headfirst position, using so much pressure that Ts'ı cried out in excruciating pain. Both agreed to try again the next day but when Ts'ı's water broke, causing her to go into labour early, it was too late to do anything about the baby's position. Ts'ı would just have to manage the labour as best she could.

In all Mamia's time delivering babies, she had only ever run into complications once where it came down to life and death. There was the real possibility of Ts'ı hemorraging or the baby being in distress and losing its heartbeat, but Mamia would never let on to Ts'ı the dangers that a breach birth posed. Instead, Mamia mentioned the doctor. "Doctor might help better," she suggested as Ts'ı struggled through the agonizing contractions that grew stronger and closer together with every minute.

Kǫ̀ looked at Mamia in worry. If Mamia thought it a good idea to call for a doctor then something must be wrong, he thought, as Ts'ı squeezed his hand tightly with each labour pain.

Their son looked worried too. Although only a few years old, he knew a baby was coming and often put his head on his mother's stomach and patted it, singing "Babia, babia." Now, as his mother cried in pain, he sat beside her trying to be as good as can be. He quietly played with a handheld toy that Kǫ̀ made for him out of a pointed caribou bone attached to a string of sinew that held a ring on the end that he threw in the air over and over trying to catch it on the end.

Again, Mamia said, "Doctor is good." Ts'ı looked surprised and creased her forehead at what Mamia was suggesting. "No. No doctor please," Ts'ı cried.

Mamia had started to doubt herself ever since she was blamed for a baby's death the year before when he had been called to help one of the local commercial fishermen's wives. When Mamia got to their small boathouse, she listened carefully for a heartbeat inside the womb but could find none. The baby had passed. It wasn't the news any parents would have wanted but there was nothing Mamia could do.

The baby's heart could have stopped beating for days and they wouldn't have known as the woman was too early in her pregnancy to feel the baby move but not early enough to miscarry without complications. She would have to give birth. Mamia's face gave away the bad news without having to say a word and the woman wept in front of her.

Her partner asked Mamia angrily as if it were her fault, "What's going on. What is it?" Mamia didn't respond, pretending not to understand him as she could see that he had been drinking. She went to work doing what she knew best for the mother to help start the process of labour by mixing an awful tasting elixir that would bring the onset of contractions. The woman gagged but drank it down, trusting that Mamia knew what she was doing.

Once the child was born, the mother wouldn't let go. No more tears fell from the mother's eyes; instead, she stared straight ahead blankly. Mamia wrapped the stillborn in a small blanket and whispered a prayer, but the woman's husband interrupted, "This is all your fault. You're some kind of a witch. I told you Susanne, we should have called the doctor. She'd still be alive. She'd still be alive, dammit." He held on gently to the child's cold blue foot only half the size of his pinky finger and looked over at Mamia, who was still in the room packing up her medicine bundle.

"Get out. Get out, you witch," he continued and Mamia did as she was told. She packed her things quickly and left but she could hear the two of them arguing all the way down the road. After that, she no longer wanted to help the townspeople. Maybe they were right, maybe the doctor had a different type of medicine that worked better than her own that could have brought the child back to life.

If that were the case, then Mamia didn't want the same thing to happen to Ts'ı. She hummed as she brushed T'si's hair out of her eyes, her strands drenched in sweat and stuck to the sides of her face. Mamia hoped that since Ts'ı had already given birth, in a relatively easy labour for a firstborn, that she would be prepared for what was to come.

Kǫ̀ and Ts'ı's baby girl was born in the middle of the night. She had been stuck in the birth canal for far too long and they all began to dread the worst. Mamia tried everything she could. She kept Ts'ı hydrated by bringing a special medicine up to Ts'ı's lips to help her relax and loosen her tense muscles while Kǫ̀ dotted her forehead and neck with cold slush from the lake.

The baby was born in late spring with a full head of dark black hair, even more than her brother, and on the very crown of her head was one noticeable thick wiry white hair standing out from the rest. The back of her neck had a generous swirl of black hair too and it couldn't hide that the baby was blue all over. When she first came out, Mamia held her close to the warmth of the woodstove and rubbed her little body firmly until the baby began to cry, and a collective relief came over the small shack by the water.

To ensure they always knew their way home, Mamia buried both of her grandchildren's umbilical cords one by one in the ground under the overhanging banks at the water's edge near their home so they would be connected to the place where they were born and never stray too far from home.

Kǫ̀ and Ts'ı held a naming ceremony for each of their children shortly after they were born as a way of reclaiming their lost language, believing that by naming their children after the land they would consider the land as a part of them. Together Ts'ı and Kǫ̀ named their children after the balance and brilliance of the earth, and both were given strong names in their own right.

Ts'ı and Kǫ̀ decided to name their son after the rock shield that spread across the northern landscape far and wide in hopes that he would be strong and steadfast throughout his life.

"He will be a shield that no one can break," Ts'ı whispered soon after their son was born as he was fast asleep in her arms.

Kǫ̀ knew that Kwe was a good name for the making of a strong man. Named after the oldest rock in the world, he would be an unbreakable force. With a name as strong as Kwe, he would be able to endure any hardship he came up against.

They chose to name their daughter Įt'ǫ̀a after the plants that flourished in the rugged wilderness in spring. From the white and yellow flowers that dotted the trails, the wild roses that overwhelmed the landscape with their picturesque beauty, to the healing powers of medicine. They hoped that through her name, Įt'ǫ̀a would grow up to be a healer like Mamia.

As a family, they did everything together. At night, they would all sit by the glow of the woodstove, telling stories about different animals like the beaver, fox and muskrat and the hard life lessons they would have to endure. The kids loved to hear Mamia's old animal stories, and they would often make fun of their father, who took on the role of making silly animal sounds.

Each morning, Kǫ̀ woke up at the same time, well before the birds began their song. He would throw enough logs into the woodstove so that his family did not have to get out of their beds and feel the cold. Once the shack was toasty warm, he would step out into the crisp morning air and see his breath no matter what time of year it was. He had found himself again, as he was in his younger days before residential school. Not a day went by that he didn't take a moment to thank Creator for his family before all else. He had reason to live. Everything he did from morning until night had a purpose far greater than himself. His family gave him purpose. He would do anything for them and wouldn't want things any other way.

Kǫ̀ was a good father. He brought his son on the land, teaching him all that he knew as soon as he was old enough to walk, as his father had done with him.

"The land is where you can always come to know your true self," Kǫ̀ said to Kwe as they both sat around the fire looking out at the stillness of the lake on one of their first hunting trips together.

"What do you mean, Dad?" his son asked curiously.

"You'll have the answers one day. Today, just listen." Kǫ̀ never lost appreciation for what his father taught him; in fact, he was surprised by how much he had come to sound like his own father.

Kǫ̀ didn't waste any time teaching his children the importance of their traditional lifestyle. His son was still so young and his daughter just a baby, but they were already learning that the land was vital to their livelihood. He wanted to give his children the chance to understand the world the way he did before his fell apart.

"The land will give you everything you need," he told his son as they warmed by the fire, but deep down Kǫ̀ had his reservations. He wasn't sure if he would be able to continue to provide for his family through hunting and trapping for much longer. His northern home was changing almost every day with the growth of the town forcing him to go further and further out to hunt, fish and trap.

Kǫ̀ was wary of teaching a way of life that might drift away for good. He had witnessed the change in the caribou herds for some time by then but as Kǫ̀ and his son ventured out further than usual on that trip, they still could not find the herd. Their narrow trails were no longer predictable like the seasonal migration patterns he once followed confidently.

"*Tıch'àadıı wenàetà-le dè, akı ɂeèzhį lade ha, hazhǫ ndè gotł'a ts'ǫ̀ ade ha,*" said Kǫ̀'s father when Kǫ̀ was a young boy as they looked out over the hill to see thousands of caribou grazing in a field. His father told him that if the caribou were not respected, they would become like ghosts on the land and disappear underground until they were respected again. Explaining that man was reliant on animals for everything — food, clothing and shelter — but that man could only take what was needed.

So when Kǫ̀ found evidence of poaching, where hunters would only take the best parts and leave the rest behind, he knew it was by the hands of those who didn't know how to hunt, who didn't know to spare an animal and use all of its parts.

For Kǫ̀, it was like walking into a crime scene finding scattered garbage blown around by the wind next to broken glass, shotgun shells and rows of bloody antlers. He would always take the time to bury the carcasses, covering the discarded parts of the animal in the freshly fallen snow. Sometimes he would try to save what he could of the leftover remains if not already scavenged. Most often what was left behind was unsalvageable, having been left to rot for far too long in the warmer seasons.

What he saw out there on the land was exactly what his father meant by not respecting the herds. The caribou were indeed becoming ghosts.

CHAPTER 9

When the time came for Kǫ̀ to bring Kwe on his first big hunt to bring down his first moose, the entire family went along.

They planned to be gone for a few weeks as Kǫ̀ got word from Woods that a large bull moose was spotted in a place where the geese would flock in the spring far from the peninsula.

Kǫ̀ figured it was likely that Woods had missed when aiming at the moose himself but would never admit it. Woods wasn't a skilled hunter by any means and Kǫ̀ didn't blame him for it; it wasn't his fault that no one taught him how.

"We leave in the morning. We'll be back in a few weeks. Make sure to keep an eye on the house," Kǫ̀ said, knowing that Woods probably wouldn't.

"Yeah, yeah, of course."

Kǫ̀ was happy to be able to bring his entire family along on the trip. Even Mamia was pleased to be going along to help take care of Įt'ǫ̀a and teach her about the different plants they would find since many of the medicines she harvested no longer grew wild in town.

Įt'ǫ̀a was still a small child, asking to be picked up and carried around in her mother's arms. Mamia being there gave Ts'ı a break from the constant duties of motherhood. Mamia took Įt'ǫ̀a on walks around the camp, teaching her the different types of plants and medicines and making it more of a game where she would show Įt'ǫ̀a a type of leaf or berry and see if Įt'ǫ̀a could find it on her own.

"The buds on the ts'ı and xochı̨̀ı̨ in the ground for pain," Mamia taught Įt'ǫ̀a as they walked together. Įt'ǫ̀a touched everything as she strolled along.

"You must be careful, some plants very strong, nàedıı̨ı̨ı," Mamia warned.

It was the time of year when the buds on the willows were getting ready to bloom — some too early, keen on opening their leaves at the first sign of spring, tricked by the warmth of the midday sun. Their budding leaves would never survive in the heavy layers of snow that still blanketed the folds in the shadows of the rock beds and under lean trees without sign of thaw.

The white lily, the most determined of the northern flowers, had already sprouted. Its thick, strong fuzzy stem somehow knowing to turn to the sun.

Įt'ǫ̀a stopped to admire the simple beauty of the lily. She crouched low to the ground and plucked one for Mamia, handing it to her happily. Mamia gave it back by tucking it under Įt'ǫ̀a's hair and around her ear, the velvet stem of it sticking to her hair.

"You are my flower, Įt'ǫ̀a," Mamia said, brushing her cheek with the back of her hand as they continued to spend the better part of the day exploring the area where they set up camp. On the other side of a small hill, they found wild sage growing out of the sand. Small mud puddles were covered in thin sheets of ice with lines and bubbles trapped inside that cracked loudly when stepped on. Įt'ǫ̀a took great interest in making sure to step on every single puddle she found before leaning over and picking a handful of sage, looking to Mamia for approval.

"This is used to heal," Mamia said as she put the bunch in her satchel that crossed over her chest and fell at her waist. They walked further until they reached an open field filled with bouquets of tall purple flowers synchronously dancing in the wind. The fireweed's long veiny stem and bright violet flowers blooming at the base by the thousands were something to be admired. "Good for tea," Mamia said.

Mamia plucked a yellow dandelion hidden under the fireweed at her feet. It had not yet turned to fluff, and she popped the yellow petals off with her thumb and ate the middle in one bite.

She plucked another one and handed it to Įt'ǫ̀a to try, but she made a funny face in return.

"Good for you," Mamia laughed. She dusted off the dandelion and swallowed it whole, rubbing her belly, "Mmm."

"Mamia," Įt'ǫ̀a said in a surprised giggle.

"You try," Mamia encouraged.

Įt'ǫ̀a looked around until she found a smaller one and tried to pop the top off with her thumb like Mamia had shown her but it was too difficult for her tiny hands to muster. She pulled off one of the silk petals and it ripped in half. She tasted a tiny piece of the broken petal with the tip of her tongue but made a sour face and threw the flower on the ground.

Mamia laughed and picked it back up, adding it to her bundle. They continued walking through the trees around their camp exploring until Įt'ǫ̀a was ready for a nap but not before Mamia found a chunk of black hardened flesh just above her head on a lone birch tree at the edge of the forest. She reached up and twisted it off before turning around and heading back to camp where she tucked Įt'ǫ̀a into bed and plunked the tłeet'ah into a pot of boiling water over the fire.

When she woke from her nap, Įt'ǫ̀a was groggy. She sat and stared straight ahead, her eyes stuck in wonder at Mamia as she watched her take turns stoking the fire and stirring what she called nàedı. Mamia saw Įt'ǫ̀a's eyes watching curiously so she looked to her and said, "This helps those who are very sick."

Meanwhile, Ts'ı was busy descaling the fish that Kwe and Kǫ̀ brought back after checking their nets. She cleaned and prepared them on the rocks by the water, then hung them to dry in a small shack made solely to hang fish and meat over the fire. At the entrance to the shack, they hung a fish head to ward off birds and land scavengers, mostly wolverines and bears.

Before Ts'ı had time to hang the fillets, Kǫ̀ and Kwe were back, sooner than expected. After just a few days they managed to come back with a moose, already skinned and quartered. They happened upon a pregnant sow and Kwe brought it down without knowing the difference while Kǫ̀ was across the way checking for fresh moose tracks. The sow just so happened to saunter in front of Kwe without noticing him and Kwe, being an opportunist, didn't wait for his father to give him the go-ahead. Kǫ̀ was impressed that Kwe shot his first moose but said, "It's okay this time because it was a moose but don't ever shoot a mother ekwǫ̀; we have to leave those ones alone."

As Kǫ̀ knew to be customary, he gave the fetus to his mother, and since Kwe would, from then on, be regarded as a good hunter, he was given the heart.

On their last day at camp before heading home, Kǫ̀ and Kwe hiked to where the slow churning river turned into quick swirling rapids, swallowing and spitting out everything that fell into its destructive path. They carefully climbed up the steep rocky slopes next to the high mist until they reached the top of the powerful waterfall.

Kǫ̀ had never seen the waterfall from the top; he had only ever seen its splendor from the bottom. For a moment he was taken aback by the thunderous, steady rush that circled together and formed a white mist that rose so high they could barely see the current pulling and snapping large pieces of driftwood in half as they fell over the side.

Kǫ̀ was so mesmerized by the waterfall that he didn't notice Kwe looking intently at something else in front of him. "What is that?" Kwe asked pointing to the other side of the falls. He tried to get a better look and moved as close to the edge as he could get without falling.

"Woah, back up," Kǫ̀ said, uneasy with how close Kwe was getting to the drop-off.

"Look, Dad." Kwe pointed to a single muskox standing statuesque on the other side of the waterfall behind the cloud of mist, staring straight at them, unafraid.

"What's it doing, Dad?"

"I don't know," Kǫ̀ said quietly, sounding almost afraid.

The muskox was an unusual animal to see in those parts, too far from the tundra. Standing alone on top of a cliff above the waterfall, it was a rare sight. Kǫ̀ didn't want to believe it, but the prophecy was coming closer. So close that he was now looking straight into the muskox's mysterious eyes for answers. When Kǫ̀ finally took his eyes off the animal he scanned the waters below. Squinting hard, he looked into the distance, trying to see if the muskox skull he saw years earlier still graced the shallows of the water but it was nowhere to be seen.

His father's words came back to him. "*Ejı̀echo eyıts'ǫ hòezıɂejı̀e deh naı̀lı̨ łak'a ts'ǫhk'e negı̨̀ıhɂà nı̨dè, ekò dè ası̀ıdeè goxè ładı̨ agode ha.*" A chill went through him. The animal was trying to tell him something, something he did not want to hear.

Looking into the glazed eyes of the muskox reflecting off the water brought him back to the bison that led him to the trail out in the far Arctic, hundreds of miles away from its grazing grounds. They were finding their way closer to each other.

When Kǫ̀ saw Kwe raise his bow and arrow to take aim at the great animal from the corner of his eye, Kǫ̀ reached out and lowered his son's arm just in time.

"No, it's trying to tell us something."

With that, the animal moved along slowly, making its way up the other side of the waterfall, balancing carefully over the steep rocks. Its broad curled horns tipped downward and to the side to move boulders out of its path as loose rocks crumbled underneath the ancient animal and fell into the waters below.

CHAPTER 10

Kǫ̀ didn't notice anything different at first, not until he got up close. He turned to Ts'ı with a million unspoken questions, but she hadn't the answers.

"Wait here," he said, and he walked a few more feet ahead stepping into the imprint of where their home once stood.

Kǫ̀ looked over his shoulder at his family who looked so small and afraid all huddled together. His mother started to say something to him, with a look of despair on her face, but he couldn't hear her. The volume in his head had turned off. Their entire world slowed to a stop.

Kǫ̀ turned every which way inspecting the surroundings with his hands on the back of his head. He crouched down and picked up a handful of cold dirt and tried not to let it slip through his fingers. He bowed his head for only a moment until he threw the rest of the earth as far as hẹ could in a demand for answers.

He wanted to be wrong, to be standing in the wrong place, but the shadows of the trees he knew so well hovered over him bending and swaying violently in the wind, as though trying to tell him what happened to his home.

Įt'ǫ̀a ran to her father and held his hand with an uncertain look, pointing doubtfully to where she knew her home should have been. She was still such a baby, Kǫ̀ thought, looking down at her innocent face. As siblings do, Kwe nudged her and told her to be quiet when he saw her face form into a frown and heard her start to whimper. To stop her from worrying, Kǫ̀ picked her up and held her, trying to remain calm for her.

Kwe held on to Mamia's hand to help her stand as her knees trembled, leaving her off balance. Without having to be told what to do, Kwe got to work quickly building a fire to keep Mamia warm while Ts'ı tended to Įt'ǫ̀a. Before they knew it, Kǫ̀ was already out of sight, on his way to Woods's house to find out what happened to their home.

As soon as Woods opened the door and saw Kǫ̀'s face he blurted, "I tried to stop them … they wouldn't listen!"

"Who's they? What are you talking about?" Kǫ̀ shouted as he grabbed Woods by the shoulders and shook him once really hard in a desperate attempt to get his home back.

"The settlers. They went to all the homes and started counting. Promising bigger houses for free. I told them to leave but they wouldn't listen. I tried to stop them Kǫ̀, but they came in with their machines."

Kǫ̀ didn't want to believe it, but despite his brother's drunkenness, he could tell that Woods was telling the truth.

Kǫ̀ let go of Woods's shoulders and backed away slowly in devastation. "I didn't ask for this." Kǫ̀ could have lived without the townspeople's interference his entire life; they may have been able to entice many of the people living on the peninsula into thinking that their way of life was better than their own way, but not Kǫ̀. Yet now he was kicking himself for not stopping it, for not knowing that somehow this was going to happen sooner or later.

He thought himself naïve to think that by staying out of their way, they would respect him enough to stay out of his. No matter what, they would have found a way to destroy what he held dear, he thought. His way of life. His happiness. His home.

That night, Kǫ̀ and Kwe worked together in silence to pitch their hunting tent in the indent where his family's house once stood. It would take a few months to rebuild, but by then, the full of winter would have set in and it would be nearly impossible for his family to camp out over the harsh winter with the kids being so young and his mother getting on in age.

Kǫ̀ could think of nowhere else to turn. Who would make room for them anyhow, he thought? Gone were the days when people in the community would help each other. Ever since the residential schools disrupted their lives, people remained guarded, nearly forgetting how to help one another and share, each family mostly to themselves.

There was always Woods's house but what he called home was no place for children with all the people coming and going and the constant drinking. With that in mind, Kǫ̀ feared the worst was yet to come.

When his family finally retired to sleep, tired out from their tears, Kǫ̀ sat outside on the cold, hard ground, looking out at the lake from where he would have once looked at it through the entryway of his home. The wind seemed to power his anger as endless rows of dark-blue white caps rolled over one another towards him. With the great lake baring its might at him, Kǫ̀ couldn't stop the storm that was coming.

By morning, the lake had calmed. Kǫ̀ forgot all about his problems as he slept, but when he woke he remembered the predicament he was in and a rage came flooding back before he could even open his eyes, and his breath escaped him all at once. His home was gone.

Pots, pans, blankets, clothing, keepsakes, all his mother's sewing supplies, gone. Everything gone. Yet it wasn't the material things that Kǫ̀ cared about. It was the look his family gave him, a look of helplessness that he couldn't fix. His children had always counted on him for protection, but this wasn't something he could save them from overnight.

The only option was to camp out until Kộ could figure out a plan for where and how they were going to rebuild their lives while all around them, homes were being built by the government on forcibly vacated lands.

After a few weeks of living in their hunting tent, a man, whom Kộ later learned was an Indian agent, showed up in the early morning. Kộ was already awake, chopping wood from the woodpile into small pieces of kindling without stopping to wipe the sweat off his brow.

"Good day," the man said taking off his black hat and exposing his shiny bald head when he spotted Kộ on the other side of the tent.

"I'm here to let you know that this area is slotted for development."

Kộ stopped what he was doing and looked up to give the man a chance to continue to explain what happened to his home before pummeling him to the ground.

"Our offices are aware of your unfortunate circumstances," the man said trying to show he cared when, in fact, he was only sticking to his orders.

Kộ walked right past the man as if he couldn't hear or see him and grabbed another log from the woodpile, nearly knocking him over as he plowed past.

"Do you speak English, sir?" the Indian agent asked slowly, condescendingly.

Kộ pulled his axe out of the stump he lodged it in and began to sharpen the blade with a shaved stone.

"The new homes will have running water and electricity …"

Still, Kǫ̀ gave no response.

"You can live in one of our newly built ones. It can be yours to own," he continued.

Only the sound of dry wood being split in half could be heard.

"I see you have children," the man kept on as he pointed to a small pair of Įt'ǫ̀a's ratty-looking moccasins that Mamia was getting around to fixing. Įt'ǫ̀a had kicked them off in a hurry to follow her mom inside from the cold and they lay just outside of the tent where Kǫ̀'s family was still sound asleep.

"Don't you ever talk about my kids," Kǫ̀ shot back, breaking his silence.

The man put his hands up in defence as Kǫ̀ took one long stride in his direction.

"Get out of here," Kǫ̀ said in a low, calculated voice.

Kǫ̀'s intimidating behaviour surprised even him, but he stood his ground with axe in hand, towering over the man. The man put his hat back on and straightened it. He pointed his chin to the sky as he turned to leave, but Kǫ̀ knew it wouldn't be the last of him.

That night, Kǫ̀ sat in silence and watched the howling winds throw the flames of his fire around wildly. He couldn't bring himself to tell Ts'ı about the man's visit. Part of him was afraid that she would want the life the agent was offering; the other part of him, his pride, didn't want her to think he had been defeated.

He pondered leaving. Packing up what little they had and starting over in the bush in T'si's birthplace. Being as secluded as it was, surely the government wouldn't want to build their fancy homes there, Kǫ̀ thought. But he knew it would be too difficult to go in the onset of winter.

It should have been the other way around, Kǫ̀ thought as he

gritted his teeth, trying to swallow the familiar rage that rose in him like the wind that stirred the flames, reminding him that winter was coming fast. How did things get to be this way? His mind ranted on with unanswered questions.

Trying to come to terms with the crossroads he was at, Kộ tried to convince himself that there would be good things about the new house. It would have more space. There would be a room for each family member. Kộ stopped himself and shook his head. He didn't care how big the house would be. His family was used to living in close quarters. Most of the time they were outside anyway. Inside was for sleeping and eating.

It really didn't matter how big or small their home was. All that mattered was that it kept them warm and safe. Their home was a place that was full of love and happiness no matter where they went, or how big or small the walls around them were, but now he feared that might all soon change.

Kộ was at odds with himself and after a few days he still hadn't told Ts'ı about the visitor, nor did he tell her that he was going to pay a visit to the housing office. He had so many things he wanted to say. So many questions. They had taken his home from him yet acted as if they were doing him a favour by offering him a place to live. It was all backwards.

He could never forgive what the government did and besides, even if he did find it in himself to forgive, there would be no apology. They tore down his home knowing someone still lived in it. Anyone could see that a family still lived there, what with all the belongings left inside. What Kộ wanted was justice.

Kộ pushed through the double doors of the housing office in the newly constructed government building that seemed to have appeared in the middle of town overnight. Its tinted windows and bright green paneling were an eyesore to Kǫ̀. He grumbled under his breath at the woman at the front desk, "I'm here about a house."

Initially, the woman at the desk was afraid of him, afraid that he might be unpredictable, though she tried her best not to show it and eased up when she learned that he was there for help.

"First and last name," the woman said flatly, her voice sounding more like an order than a question.

Just then a deep voice boomed out of the office behind the woman's desk. The office door was half open and inside a large man paced with a cigarette in hand while talking on the phone. He seemed to be laughing about "lot sizes" as he walked confidently from one corner of his office to the other across the tacky, carpeted flooring, the mustard yellow phone cord dragging behind him.

The woman cleared her throat to get Kǫ̀'s attention.

"Name," she said again as she sat under a picture of a fenced-in horse next to an old barn, a place somewhere far away from the North, Kǫ̀ thought. Her desk was covered in stacks of papers.

The need to produce a name forced Kǫ̀ into a whole new dilemma. If he gave his real name, it would be giving even more of himself away. So he buckled down and took on his imposter name.

"Christian Collins."

"Sign here," she said as she pushed the papers over to Kǫ̀.

He stared at the dark line on the paper below a bunch of scrambled letters and a big letter X where he was to sign. Kǫ̀ tried to adjust his eyes. He never did learn to read in school; he couldn't even sound out the words if he tried. It wasn't that he couldn't understand; it was that he didn't want to. Besides, everything he learned in school had left his mind the second he was free.

The woman behind the bulky desk could see that Kộ couldn't comprehend the words on the paper when he rubbed his eyes.

"You're not signing anything important, just agreeing to live in a new home that you'll eventually own," she grinned, the stone-face lie not quite hidden. Her smile captured the picture of greed as a confident look of entitlement spread across her face when she saw that he was being cooperative by picking up the pen.

"Sign here," she pointed, all too eager to exert authority, as though she had power over him, and, in a way, maybe she did, Kộ thought.

CHAPTER 11

The government wasted no time building dozens of "new and improved" homes on the peninsula, crowding the limited open spaces even further on the encroached lands they claimed. They drilled, sawed and banged their hammers from morning until night building large two-storey homes that sat on top of concrete blocks. They had a different man for each job. One to hook up the pipes, one to hook up the wires, one to stuff pink fluffy insulation in between two-by-fours held together with glue, hammers and nails, and one to put the shingles on the rooftops. They were up and down ladders with saws hanging from tool belts and dull pencils behind their ears.

As Kộ walked past their worksites, he grumbled to himself. Everything they did was unnatural. It all had to first be put through a machine. It was all made from some kind of metal or plastic, everything created by man. Kộ could hear them swearing crudely from inside the tent; there was no escape from the noise except when the men finally took a break for lunch.

"Hello? ... Mr. Collins?" The short bald man was back again. This time, the agent was armed with a clipboard and pen in hand. He struggled to find the entrance to the tent, a seam tied from the inside. The man slapped the tent cloth annoyingly several times, having given up on trying to find the opening.

"Mr. Collins, are you in there?" The man put his ear closer to listen inside.

Kǫ̀ knew the small man was back the second he stepped foot out of his government car that rolled up on the big gravel chunks just a few feet from their tent. The exhaust fumes weren't enough to stop Kǫ̀ from taking his time finishing breakfast as he ignored the man's pesky voice, but Į̀t'ǫ̀a ran out of the tent to see who it was. When she saw the man leaning, trying to listen in, she kicked him hard in the shins. The man jumped around on one foot in pain and, although a devout Catholic, it didn't stop him from yelling, "Jesus Christ."

Ts'ı followed Į̀t'ǫ̀a outside, "Į̀t'ǫ̀a!" she called and brought her back inside holding her by the wrist, her arm stretched high to her mother's side. Kwe smiled at his sister in approval as he sat beside his father eating a bowl of oats mixed with fried caribou meat.

"Your house is ready," the man said begrudgingly, rubbing his bruising leg.

"I've come to do a walk-through with you." He dangled a set of keys the same way that Kǫ̀ dangled scraps of meat to his sled dogs when he was a boy.

"We don't need you to walk us anywhere," Kǫ̀ said, his voice deep, as he met the man outside the tent, towering over him threateningly.

"Well, alright then. Here you are."

Before the man could hand the keys over, Kǫ̀ swiped them out of his hand. They locked eyes, neither one of them looking away as if playing a game of chicken. Giving up on the expectation of a thank you, the man backed up slowly to put more distance between himself and an unpredictable Kǫ̀.

"Well, then, if you have any questions, I believe you know where our offices are located," the small man said as he walked away loosening his button-up collar.

Winter had seemed to wait for them that year as it had come later than usual. The first snowfall never stayed for long; it would always melt after a few days. This time, although late, the first snowfall was there to stay, covering everything under a thick heavy white canvas.

One by one, with Kǫ̀ trailing reluctantly behind, his small family walked up the steep stairs to the front door. Ts'ı held onto Mamia's arm to help her up the slippery steps. Kǫ̀ looked over his shoulder one last time at the vacant parcel of land slotted for development where he had the painstaking task of taking his tent down that morning, hoping that the only home he ever knew would miraculously reappear so that he wouldn't have to walk one step further into the new undesirable house he couldn't imaging living and dying in.

When the door shut behind them, sealing them in, a cloud of darkness fell on them or maybe it was just the way the light was kept out with too many walls and not enough windows. They were, for the most part, a quiet family, but this newfound silence filled the air with unanswered questions and a deep concern for what the future would hold.

The house looked like a large cardboard box. A perfect square. Every room was empty and hollow, leaving nothing but an echo of their footsteps hanging in the air. Kǫ̀ knew the moment he stepped foot in the door that he would never call it home.

Aside from Ts'ı, it was the first time in their lives, they had running water, flushing toilets and electricity. There was no place to burn wood, no cellar for storing food for the winter and no honey bucket out back, which was the only thing they wouldn't miss.

Kǫ̀ supposed that most people would be grateful for being given a house, but he could never muster up the gratitude even if he tried. It was in the way it had come about. Without consent. Nevertheless, he had no other choice but to play by the rules of the game, to live in the confines of the government's regime. With the shutting of the door, he felt as though he had turned his back on the land he truly called home.

For the first year, they all slept on the floor in the same room on top of their furs. But even the soft furs couldn't keep their backs from hurting on the uncomfortable cold, hard laminate floor unlike the soft beds of spruce bough Kǫ̀ once spread out on the ground, nature's cushion.

Although Ts'ı was familiar with using a stove, she still preferred to cook outside and continued to use the fire pit near the lake. They all agreed that freshly plucked and singed geese would never taste as good on the stove as it did over the fire. In fact, Ts'ı, Kǫ̀ and Mamia had collectively opted out of using most of the appliances that came with the house except for the refrigerator. Ts'ı continued to wash their clothes in the lake in the summer and hung them on a line to dry.

Kwe couldn't understand why his parents weren't taking the time to learn how to use the new appliances as he could see that it would have made their lives much easier. It was through Kwe's reaction to his parents' refusal to use the modern luxuries that Kǫ̀ first noticed the impact living in the house was having on his son.

Kwe quickly got used to easy living and seemed to enjoy it, which made Kǫ̀ despise the conveniences of the house even more. The things that were supposed to be making their lives easier were instead filling their lives with idleness, and for the first time in his life, Kǫ̀ had to scold Kwe for not helping his mother with chores.

But Kwe was downright amazed and preoccupied with the second-hand bulky black-and-white television encased in wood and a crooked set of antennas. The tv was given to them by a woman that Ts'ı worked with at her new cleaning job but Kǫ̀ had no use for it and refused to even look at it.

"Look at him. It's making him lazy." Kǫ̀ stated his case to Ts'ı in the kitchen as he looked over at his son sitting on the floor cross-legged and staring at the tv a few inches in front of his face.

"He's not doing anything wrong. Just leave him," Ts'ı said, defending him.

"He's not doing anything is what he's doing," Kǫ̀ said.

"He's done his chores," Ts'ı quipped.

"Well give him more then."

"Like what they made us do at school?"

"Not like that," Kǫ̀ stammered.

"What else should he be doing?"

"Just never mind," Kǫ̀ said.

Ts'ı just rolled her eyes.

"See now that thing is coming in between us too," he said as he pointed at the tv.

"This has nothing to do with the tv," Ts'ı said as he walked away.

"Let's go check the traps for rabbits," Kǫ̀ said to his son after breakfast one morning on one of Kǫ̀'s rare days off. Kwe had already taken up his regular spot in front of the tv and didn't hear his father; he didn't even budge.

Kǫ̀ spoke in a louder, firmer tone.

"Kwe. Get ready, we're going to check traps."

Still, Kwe didn't even look in his father's direction, too transfixed by the obnoxious shows. Kǫ̀ wanted to rip the cord from the wall and chuck the box down the steep front steps, but it wouldn't have helped. It would only have made him look even that much more desperate to control what was rapidly getting away from him. He was losing a battle that he wasn't sure he could win.

Kǫ̀ knew the only way to ensure Kwe wasn't completely lost to the kwet'ı̨̀ı̨ way of living was to bring him out on the land. From day one of living in the house, Kǫ̀ had wanted nothing more than to get back to nature, but after all that time he still had no means of travelling long distances in the winter and walked everywhere. He knew Ts'ı wouldn't want him to take Kwe too far on foot. So when he found out that Woods had come into some skidoos of his own, he didn't hesitate to ask his brother if he could borrow them.

Kǫ̀ was at such a loss, desperate to spend time on the land with his son that he turned a blind eye to Woods's dealings, not wanting to know the details of how his brother got the machines in the first place. He heard that Woods had given up on bootlegging after being fined one too many times, but he hadn't been working a steady job either. In fact, the last time they spoke, Woods had mentioned something about someone owing him money.

Kǫ̀ didn't want to know about where or how Woods got his money. His guilt would get in the way of him borrowing the skidoos if he knew that Woods had bought them illegitimately. It mattered to him if the skidoos were bought with the money from the sale of drugs or booze sold into the community after seeing what it did to Woods and so many others. Either way, Kǫ̀ was lying to himself by turning away from knowing the truth and going ahead with his plan.

Deep into the trails, the freshly fallen snow covered the trees, making everything sparkle like diamonds wherever the short winter sunlight shined down. Kwe stood up on the skidoo every time a branch was close enough for him to reach and big chunks of piled-up snow slipped off and fell onto his father's head, who was following closely behind. Kǫ̀ didn't mind; it was the first time that he had a reason to smile since being in the new house. Kwe's seeming playfulness made Kǫ̀ feel lighthearted, but little did he know that Kwe was doing it out of spite for having to accompany his father unwillingly.

After setting the soft-wired traps that they would check on their return, they stopped and built a fire at the edge of one of the smaller ponds between the trails to take a break. Kǫ̀ sat back and opened a can of mixed fruit with his hunting knife as part of the lunch that Ts'ı had lovingly packed for them.

"These trails have been used by your ancestors for thousands of years. You know that, right?"

Kwe nodded and partially rolled his eyes expecting his dad to go on one of his spiels that he had told countless times but instead he said, "Once we get a bit further ahead, the lakes are going to get smaller and smaller, until we reach the lake where the fish swims like a snake." Kǫ̀ moved his hand side to side mimicking the motion of the fish for Kwe.

"That's where we'll stop for the night. The trails up this way are full of overflow. We need to drive through them quickly so we don't get stuck in it. So, follow me closely," he said and handed Kwe the rest of the half-empty can of fruit.

Kwe nodded and ate what was left, drinking up the syrup at the bottom that he wished accompanied a piece of toast like Mamia usually made for him to dip it in and soak up the juice. Kwe wasn't really listening to his father; he was daydreaming about being wrapped up in his blanket in front of the television, more interested in getting back to the comforts of being indoors. He didn't understand the importance of being out in the cold, not when he could be warm inside at home watching his favourite shows.

Kǫ̀ dumped a large clump of snow onto the fire to put it out and it let out a long, drawn-out sizzle. In no time, they were on their way again to where the trail narrowed and went down a steep slope that led them deep into the trees. Kǫ̀ warned Kwe that if they weren't careful to keep their legs and arms tucked in, they could break a bone by hitting it on one of the trees. Kwe rode his brakes behind his dad like he was taught, but at the bottom they were at a crossroad where the trail split in two directions.

Kǫ̀ took to the right and looked back at Kwe, who was no more than a few yards behind him. He waved and pointed to the trail he was about to go down to make sure that Kwe knew which way to go. Kwe nodded, and Kǫ̀ took it as an indication that he knew to follow, but Kwe was just fixing his oversized helmet to keep it from falling forward. When he could finally see better, he veered to the left instead, going down the wrong trail, a trail only used by expert trappers and fishermen.

After a few minutes, Kǫ̀ looked behind him to check on Kwe but saw no sign of him. Kǫ̀ slowed and listened for the sound of Kwe's skidoo, but the sound of his machine was too loud. Kǫ̀ turned off the skidoo and jumped off to listen but heard nothing. He trudged through the snow and backtracked down the trail, still listening for Kwe. He picked up on the buzzing sound of Kwe's engine but it was so far away that it sounded as quiet as a mosquito buzzing around his head.

Kwe was, by then, far down the wrong trail and going faster and faster to try and catch up to his dad, not knowing he had gone in the wrong direction. Kǫ̀ ran back to his skidoo and lifted the heavy back end of the machine to turn it around. He worked quickly knowing that he was losing time. The trail Kwe was on led to a small lake with open water from the constant flow of the rapids. He needed to get to Kwe before it was too late.

Kǫ̀ revved the skidoo engine full force. In his hurry, he shot the front end of the skidoo up in the air. He throttled the machine as fast as it would allow but his inexperience in operating the clunky skidoo soon found him wrapped around a tree.

"No," he yelled in a panic.

He got off and struggled to untangle the skis from the roots and the skidoo vibrated and gave off a thick cloud of smoke.

"Kwe!" he cried out for his son in vain, still trying to pull the skidoo free from the tree.

Kǫ̀ tried not to think about what could happen if Kwe reached the water as he worked quickly to get the skidoo back on track. The more he tried to free the skis, the harder it seemed. Only when he looked to Creator for help did he become calm enough to get the skidoo unstuck.

Going down the wrong trail felt like an endless nightmare as he thought of the worse that could happen. Kǫ̀ grew more afraid at every turn with no sign of Kwe except the fresh tracks he left behind. When Kǫ̀ finally made it to the end of the trail, he saw Kwe's skidoo tracks leading straight out onto the ice close to the open water. Without slowing, Kǫ̀ drove out onto the semi-frozen river before him but there was no sign of Kwe or the skidoo. Kǫ̀ stood up on the skidoo while driving and scanned the open water. Amidst rows of long sharp icicles bobbing up and down on an angle, he saw something dark move at the far end of the rapids just for a second and his heart nearly went through his chest.

Kwe had gone under.

By the time Kǫ̀ got to him, Kwe was barely hanging onto a thin sheet of ice that shouldn't have been strong enough to keep him from being dragged into the swirling current but by some miracle it was. The skidoo already long sunk to the bottom.

"Don't let go," Kǫ̀ yelled, getting as close as he could before jumping off the moving skidoo and breaking into a run. He grabbed a rope from his bag that he always carried with him for emergencies, and raced towards Kwe. Each step he took was wasted time as his heavy boots broke through the light crust on the surface of the deep snow. At any moment he too expected to go under so he got down on his stomach and crawled towards

Kwe. When he got as close as possible without falling in, on his elbows, he dragged his legs behind him to make himself as light as he could.

"Grab the rope," he yelled over the sound of the moving water between them. Kwe tried to grab the rope but it fell into the water a few feet from his reach and he slipped further to his demise with one arm slapping the surface and he flailed as his legs were pulled by the current flowing under the ice.

"Try to stay calm."

Kǫ̀ could see Kwe was beginning to go into shock, his lips blue. They didn't have much time. Kǫ̀ pulled the rope back in and tossed it out again. This time Kwe caught the frayed end and with what little strength he had left, he trusted his father and let go. The ice that he held onto for his life instantly broke off and was carried away with the current, the beaded mitts Mamia made swept away with it.

Kǫ̀ carried Kwe to the shoreline in a hurry and sat him under a large spruce tree where fluffs of snow fell on his head only it wasn't funny. Kwe shivered uncontrollably while Kǫ̀ worked fast to start a fire, digging a deep hole in the ground, shoveling out the snow with both his hands like a dog digging for a bone.

Kǫ̀ worked madly, grabbing the driest branches he could find at the bottom of the tree, snapping them into small pieces and piling them up on top of each other in the shape of a square, leaving just enough room for pockets of air to get in between to fan the flame.

Kǫ̀ removed Kwe's wet clothes and replaced them with his own until Kǫ̀ was left half-naked. The wind hit him fiercely, leaving his skin with large red and white blotches, but all he cared about was that Kwe was warm. Kǫ̀ rubbed Kwe all over his body to get his blood flowing again. He didn't stop until the colour of his lips turned a lighter shade of blue; only then did he know he would be okay. At any rate, they wouldn't make it back home before nightfall. Kwe was in no shape to leave the warmth of the fire. They would have to wait until morning.

"I can't feel my fingers," Kwe cried.

"Keep moving them. Your toes too."

Kǫ̀ tried to get Kwe to redirect his thoughts.

"Mom's going to be worried sick about you. She's probably got supper on the table."

Kwe looked like he was falling asleep, his eyes rolling backwards.

Kǫ̀ shook him and roughed up his hair. "If she were here right now, she'd already have a big cup of hot chocolate and marshmallows for you," Kǫ̀ said, trying to keep him awake.

"Dad," Kwe cried with what little energy he had left to speak, shivering so much that his teeth chattered violently.

"What? What is it?" Kǫ̀ rubbed his son's shoulders and arms, creating warmth from the friction.

"I want to go home."

"I know, son, it's okay, I'll get you home." Kwe's pleading words hit Kǫ̀ hard in the gut. He had met his defeat, for to him, they were already home.

CHAPTER 12

Life had become routine. Monotonous. Structured. Then just like that one day it was interupted when Įt'ǫ̀a answered a knock on the door to see a tall woman wearing a black suit with a briefcase at her side.

"Hi there, are your parent's home?" The woman looked down at Įt'ǫ̀a who looked back at her with a sideways glance. Without a word, she slammed the door and ran to tell her father.

"There's someone at the door for you." Įt'ǫ̀a said to Kǫ̀ who was home early from work sitting at the kitchen table drinking a tall glass of tap water in his work boots.

Kǫ̀ slowly made his way to the door. He took one look at the woman and knew she had nothing good to say.

"What do you want?" he asked without inviting the woman in, even though she looked cold.

"May I come in?"

He begrudgingly opened the door wider and stepped back to let her in.

"Mr. Collins, I've been asked to deliver a paper to you regarding your mother …" She squinted at the white sheet, unsure of how to pronounce the spelling of his mother's name.

"My mother? What do you want with her?" he asked defensively.

"Well, sir, she will need to be placed into a home. There are only enough bedrooms in this house for your immediate family."

"Immediate family? What do you mean my immediate family? My mother's as immediate as it gets," he said raising his voice.

"I'm sorry, sir, but you aren't allowed to have this many people living in one home. It says so in the agreement you signed. I have a copy right here." She handed him the paper but Kǫ̀ tore it up and she watched the pieces fall to the floor at her feet.

"I don't care what I signed. She's not going anywhere, but you are," he said sharply and moved towards the door to show her out.

"Sir, no need to get upset. You'll have to take it up with headquarters. I'm sure you know where our offices are," she said in a patronizing tone as she walked out on her own accord.

Ts'ı had been listening in on the conversation around the corner at the end of the hall. Mamia was taking a late afternoon nap, sleeping soundly on a thin single bed in the living room made up of piled-up blankets while Įt'ǫ̀a sat at her feet drawing pictures of flowers.

"What are we going to do?" Ts'ı asked anxiously. "She can't go into a home. She won't be happy there. We are her family. This is her home." She whispered in case Mamia woke and overheard them talking.

"She's not going anywhere," Kǫ̀ said as he put his jacket on.

Kǫ̀ walked up the hill to Coppertown in the blowing snow. The dirt roads, once covered in large chunks of gravel and salt had since been replaced with pavement and painted yellow lines.

By the time he reached the housing office, he couldn't feel his legs. The second he walked into the warm building they burned with an intense stinging sensation. The same woman sat behind the desk,; each time he saw her, her hair was a bit greyer than the last.

"Christian, how can I help you today?" the woman asked facedly. She and Kǫ̀ had come to know each other over the years through his constant complaints.

"Let me talk to Walters," Kộ said impatiently.

"I'm afraid he's busy at the moment," she lied.

"I'll wait," Kộ said and sat down on the chair next to her desk.

The woman uncomfortably shifted in her seat and called her boss on the intercom. "Mr. Walters, Christian's here to see you again … um . . . hmm … yes … uh huh."

"You can go in," she said tersely.

Kộ walked into Walter's office without knocking.

"Mr. Collins, how can I help you today? Everything alright with the house?" he asked, knowing full well what Kộ was there for as he leaned far back into his leather twirling chair flicking the pen in his hand.

"No. Everything's not alright with the house. You know damn well what I'm here for. I want to know why one of your people came to tell me my mother can't live with us anymore," Kộ demanded.

"Mr. Collins, I know you're upset, but that is what is stated clearly in the agreement you signed. There's no room for your mother in that house. Besides, don't you think she'd be happier if she had her own space?" The first two buttons on his white collared shirt were unbuttoned and Kộ couldn't help but notice the few sparse long wisps of reddish blonde hair tangled into a gold chain on which a small cross hung.

"No! She's fine where she is."

"Well, then, you would be breaking your contract, which means the land and house'll have to be turned back into our possession," Mr. Walters said matter of fact.

"Back? It was never yours to begin with. I never agreed to this. If I knew this was going to happen …" Kộ rose in the chair and it fell backwards onto the floor.

"Calm down, Collins. Just think about it. The seniors' home is a comfortable facility. Your mother'll be living with people her own age, taken care of by a health care professional. It's for the best," he said, now sitting straight up and on guard in his chair.

"Would you put your own mother in a place like that?"

"Mr. Collins, my mother died a long time ago. The receptionist will fill you in on the details on your way out," he said coldly. Looking past Kǫ̀, he hollered, "Nora, give him the brochure, will you?"

"They call it an old folks home. Old lady Therese has been there for a while now, and she seems to like it," Ts'ı said to Kǫ̀ later that evening as she poured him a warm cup of tea to ease his troubled mind.

"I don't care what they call it. She's not going. We need her and she needs us," he said.

"I don't want to see her go either, Kǫ̀, but what other choice do we have?"

Kǫ̀'s mother had been pretending to sleep, listening to them talk. When she finally had enough, she got up and walked over to them with one hand resting on her aching hip.

"I will go," she said assertively.

"Pour me some tea, my dear." She joined Kǫ̀ at the kitchen table, putting her hand on his. "I don't want to hear the two of you argue. You never argued before we moved, into this … this place."

Ts'ı handed her the tea and she put the steaming cup to her lips. "Sìı whekǫ̀," she said putting the teacup back down on the table.

"You never know, I might like it there. Some of my friends are there. I will go and that's the last of it."

Saying goodbye to Mamia was abrupt. The move happened so

fast that Kwe and Įt'ǫ̀a didn't have time to let it sink in. When Woods came to pick her up and drive her down the road to the old folks home, Kwe was able to keep his composure but Įt'ǫ̀a cried miserably as they took turns hugging Mamia. Kwe gave her his favourite piece of shale rock in the shape of a heart and Įt'ǫ̀a gave her a picture she drew of a yellow dandelion.

Įt'ǫ̀a held onto Mamia's suitcase and wouldn't let it go when Woods tried to pull it out of her hand. He had to tug on it to free it from her strong grip. It was then that Ts'ı saw how close Įt'ǫ̀a was to Mamia, maybe even closer than they were to each other.

"Do you remember when you were small you used to hold onto Mamia's leg wherever she went?" Ts'ı put her arm around Įt'ǫ̀a as they watched Woods help her into his dusty truck.

"Do you remember how she nursed you back to health when you got sick? You were so small you probably don't remember," Ts'ı said in a comforting tone.

"I remember," Įt'ǫ̀a said, wiping her tears with her sleeve.

"You were so sick; we didn't know what to do but Mamia did."

"Why are you letting her leave? Who's going to help her? She's going to be all alone," Įt'ǫ̀a said.

"We didn't have a choice, Įt'ǫ̀a," Ts'ı said looking at Kǫ̀ for help, but he was helping load the last of Mamia's luggage in the back of the pickup.

"Yeah. Įt'ǫ̀a's right. She took care of us. Now it's our turn to care of her," Kwe said.

Ts'ı didn't know what to say to make things easier. Įt'ǫ̀a shrugged free of her mother's arm and went to her room to cry into her pillow.

"You're going to be okay, babia," Mamia said as she patted her back.

"Snow bad," Įt'ǫ̀a said.

Mamia was confused. "Ayìı?"

Įt'ǫ̀a coughed, weak and pale with sickness.

"Snow blegghh," she said and pointed out the window at the lake. "I don't eat snow no more."

"Here babia, drink." Mamia sat her up and gave her another sip of warm broth. "This has all the plants and flowers we picked, remember? Its going to help heal you," Mamia said trying to make her feel better.

"Yummy flowers," Įt'ǫ̀a said trying to force a smile through her burning fever.

When Įt'ǫ̀a fell asleep that night, Mamia told Kǫ̀ and Ts'ı what Įt'ǫ̀a told her about the snow.

"Did you know Įt'ǫ̀a ate snow out back?"

"What?" Kǫ̀ asked.

"She said the snow behind the house had a funny taste," Mamia explained.

"Come to think of it, she was playing near the lake making a snowman with Kwe before she got sick," Ts'ı said worriedly.

Kwe was outside sliding down a small snow mound on a piece of cardboard with his friends just off the side of the road when Kǫ̀ called him in from the open kitchen window. "Kwe jǫ̀ıtłe."

"How are you feeling Kwe?" Mamia asked as he walked into house, stopping on the mat, the snow on his boots forming a puddle. She checked his forehead.

"Fine," he said. He was sweaty and huffing, his nose dripping with snot and his cheeks bright red from running around outside in the cold air.

"Was your sister eating snow the other day when you were making that snowman behind the house?" Ts'ı asked.

"Yeah, I told her not to but she still did it anyway. I told her it had dog pee on it," he said with a laugh.

"You didn't eat any snow though?" Kǫ̀ asked.

"No, ew," Kwe said. "It really was yellow. Can I go now? My friends are waiting for me," he whined.

"If Kwe's not sick and none of us are sick it can't be the flu," Ts'ı said.

"I used to eat snow all the time when I was a kid and never got sick. It's from the people up the hill is what it is."

"She's going to be okay. She just needs rest," Mamia said.

Kǫ̀ promised Mamia that they would visit every day, but the visits were never long enough. When they did visit, they only had a small window of time as visiting hours were kept short. Mamia grew old fast without her grandchildren around to keep her young.

The most vital member of their family had been forcefully removed in a way that was accepted by a society not their own. She had not died, but yet they were in mourning and the house had become cold overnight without her in it.

Kwe and Įt'ǫ̀a missed her soft voice, her kind eyes, her gentle smile, her patience and the way she patted their backs and softly hummed songs until they fell asleep. Ts'ı tried to pick up the pieces after Mamia left to fill the empty spaces in the house but she was so busy with her part-time job in the evenings at the local doctor's office and washing dishes at the restaurant day to day. She and Kǫ̀ had to work double shifts to bring in enough money to keep up with their bills and put food on the table.

Ts'ı brought Įt'ǫ̀a along to work with her most evenings at the doctor's office, where she played with the medical equipment in the supply room and pretended to be a doctor, putting on blue gloves and mask and using prescription papers she found in a box on a shelf to scribble on while her mom vacuumed and scrubbed the toilets.

By then, Kǫ̀ was always working late hours at the mine. He had to completely give up hunting and trapping and get a job to pay the mortgage and the bills that came as part of the agreement that he signed. Kǫ̀ got a job as a labourer at the local gold mine where he worked hundreds of feet underground in a cold damp cave dripping with arsenic.

Even with a steady job, Kǫ̀ still worried about making enough money. Before moving into the house, he never had to work for money. Work to him meant going out on the land and providing for his family the way his father had taught him. It was never about personal gain. Now, he was working to pay bills to put store-bought food on the table, replacing the traditionally harvested meals they once enjoyed as a family with expensive food that gave him heartburn.

With little to no time to go out on the land and hunt, Kǫ̀ was never able to fill their freezer with meat. The only time they ever had wild meat was when it was given to them by Chief and Council. It had come to the point where community sharing became so limited that people became secretive about how much meat they had stored away.

Sharing had been a big part of the community when Kǫ̀ was a child. He remembered how the families on the peninsula had shared everything they had with one another, but now that money had become a central part of their lives, sharing was replaced with hoarding.

Kǫ̀ and Ts'ı had no choice but to work so that they could afford to pay for the unnecessary comforts that neither of them had asked for. Kǫ̀ could have gone the rest of his life without money as a source of livelihood, but now he was stuck having to work at a job that plundered the land in order to live on his own territory. It just didn't make sense to him. The lifestyle Kǫ̀ remembered, unencumbered by money, was in the past.

CHAPTER 13

Over the years, the house began to fall apart all around them. It was poorly built to begin with, having been put together nearly overnight. After placing one too many maintenance orders that went unanswered, Kǫ̀ gave up relying on the housing office to fill his requests and began fixing the house up himself with what little money he and Ts'ı had been able to save.

Kǫ̀ fixed the leaks and drafts as best he could, but he couldn't keep up with the endless problems that the house presented. Not able to withstand the winters, the house had become so run down that it wasn't worth putting money into fixing up, but he did what little he could to keep it from falling down.

Not one day went by that Kǫ̀ didn't miss the old way of living on the land. He still had full intentions of rebuilding a cabin for his family out in the bush one day but just didn't have the time or energy to start making his dream a reality after working long hard hours day in and day out just to turn around and put it into the house. Each day his dream of one day living back out on the land again drifted further and further away from him.

It was the Christmas that their power bill got so high that things really started taking a turn for the worse. Even with the money that Kǫ̀ and Ts'ı had saved up, they still had to make the difficult choice of paying their monthly power bill over purchasing Christmas presents.

"They'll be the only kids without presents. We don't even have a tree." Ts'ı had a very difficult time coming to terms with the fact that Kwe and Įt'ǫ̀a would wake up on Christmas morning and have no presents when she knew that other children their age would have got presents from Santa, a Christmas tree and stockings full of candy.

It wasn't easy, but Ts'ı managed to talk Kǫ̀ into waiting to pay the power bill until after Christmas.

"It's either that or I take on more shifts," Ts'ı protested, knowing that working even more was not something that Kǫ̀ would have wanted for her seeing how exhausted Ts'ı was.

"What is it with you and Christmas anyway? It's not our way. We never celebrated Christmas." Christmas was not a time of joy for Kǫ̀. It was a reminder that he wasn't allowed to go home while some kids were. Christmas was not in his vocabulary.

Ts'ı didn't want to start going down the old familiar road of arguing over religion. Unlike Kǫ̀, she believed that Jesus was a prophet, a real person who had gifts like Mamia. She believed that the land was Creator of all things, but she also held on to what she was taught in Sunday school. They were divided in their beliefs, and religion became an ongoing point of contention between them. It was an argument that was never won and so they tried to veer away from bringing it up, but it was impossible not to with Christmas just around the corner.

Ts'ı even tried compromising. "Maybe instead of taking extra shifts I can try my luck at bingo? A few of the girls have been playing at the Friendship Centre every Saturday. Bessie won five hundred dollars on a pull ticket last weekend," Ts'ı said excitedly.

"Gambling? That's your solution?" Kǫ̀ asked, one eyebrow raised.

"It's just a thought. You never know, I might win," Ts'ı said, not needing his permission but hoping he would get on board with the idea.

"Sure, and I'll just start bootlegging with Woods too and get thrown in jail and lose my job," Kǫ̀ said in what was quite possibly the first time he had ever brought sarcasm into their relationship.

"How can you compare bingo to bootlegging?" Ts'ı asked, now irritated.

"Because both are risks we can't take. Spending what you have in hopes you might win and when, *if*, you do you'll just end up spending more to lose the next time. Then you'll keep playing until you win again. It's a trap, Ts'ı," Kǫ̀ fired back but Ts'ı was already down the hallway on her way to the bedroom, walking away from the argument that had been brewing since December rolled around.

Little did Kǫ̀ know that she had already been dabbling in gambling. With the money she had leftover from her paycheques, Ts'ı was purchasing scratch tickets in hopes that she might win enough money to help pay the bills and even better, buy more than one Christmas present each for Į̨t'ǫ̀a and Kwe. She didn't mean for it to be a secret from Kǫ̀ but now that she knew where he stood on gambling, she wasn't going to let on that she was playing scratchies or he would definitely think she had a problem.

In their room, Ts'ı hid the saved tickets under the mattress. With her tendency to hold onto things, a habit that was brought on by losing almost everything she had as a child, she saved every single scratch ticket, even the ones that weren't winners.

Kǫ̀ couldn't remember the last time December was so cold other than the first winter he had spent at the school. They turned up the heat more than usual to keep the house warm, even having to resort to using the kitchen stove, but the weather didn't stop the housing office from exercising their ruthless tyranny. Without warning, the switch to their power was turned off just one day after their power bill was late. It wasn't the first time it had happened. They had their power shut off a couple of times in the warmer months, but this time though, it meant life or death.

"What is this? Three strikes you're out?" Kǫ̀ said looking up at the ceiling. Ts'ı couldn't tell if he was talking out loud to God or the power company.

With no heat from the furnace, the pipes froze and burst in a matter of a few hours, flooding the ground underneath the house in a yellow overflow that formed a frozen pond. With no woodstove to keep them warm, they were completely reliant on the power company.

Ts'ı piled up blanket after blanket and they all huddled together on the couch in the cold, dark house. Kwe and Įt'ǫ̀a soon fell asleep sitting up, side by side, their brown strands of hair mixed together, so cold they couldn't move.

"This is what we get for trying to celebrate Christmas? Where's the mercy?" Kǫ̀ griped.

"Sshh, you'll wake the kids," Ts'ı said quietly. "You're just going to have to go down to the housing office tomorrow and ask them to turn the heat back on. They have to turn it back on. Right?"

Kǫ̀ nodded to ease her mind.

Kǫ̀ paced outside the housing office so early the next morning that the employees assumed he was homeless as they shuffled in. He got no sleep. Nowhere could he find relief from the cold. The power plant was on the outskirts of town, so he thought he'd first try talking to Walters, who seemed to control more than he let on.

Kǫ̀ confronted Walters in the parking lot as he got out of his car. "You promised me the house would be free. My kids are freezing up in that dump that you built," Kǫ̀ said as he approached Walters, blowing into his fists to keep them warm.

"Christian. Good morning to you too. Let's get out of the cold first, then we talk," Walters said, grabbing his briefcase from the backseat.

Once inside, Nora brought Walters his steaming morning cup of coffee as he hung his jacket on the wooden coat rack.

"The papers you signed were for home ownership. If that's not something that you feel comfortable with, we can always move you into a rental agreement. You won't have to pay any bills; just a small portion of the rent. We know you're struggling to make ends meet Christian. This'll take the pressure off," Walters explained in one long fed-up exhale.

Walters slid a piece of paper across the desk and told Kǫ̀ where to sign. Kǫ̀ fought the urge to tear up the paper when he saw it but then remembered what Ts'ı said.

"All you have to do is sign and we'll lower the rent." Kǫ̀ could have sworn he saw a grin on Walters' face.

"What about my power?"

"Well, the power we don't control. That's the power company but I can make sure they turn it back on for you."

"Right now. Do it now," Kǫ̀ demanded.

"Right now?"

"Now," Kǫ̀ shouted, his body still shaking from being cold for too long.

"Nora, get the power corp on the line, will you," Walters said, not taking his eyes off Kǫ̀.

"There, are you happy? You can relax now."

Kǫ̀ looked behind him and watched to make sure Nora picked up the phone.

"You can go back out on the land again. You won't have to work so hard to pay the bills. I know how much you love the land, Christian. When's the last time you were able to get out there?" Walters asked.

It all still sounded too good to be true to Kǫ̀, and he stood like a stone waiting to hear what else Walters would come up with.

"You won't need to pay as much money anymore. The rent will be at an affordable set rate. We'll turn the power back on once you sign. Do you understand what I'm saying?" Walters looked up at Kǫ̀ with a squint, waiting for an answer.

Kǫ̀ thought of what this might mean for his family. Ts'ı would be able to quit her evening job and spend more time at home with the kids. They both wouldn't have to work so hard to pay bills. He could go back out on the land and start building a cabin so they could get out of housing once and for all.

He looked at Walters who was beginning to turn red in the face as if he were holding his breath waiting for a response. Either that or he was near ready for a heart attack. Kǫ̀ picked up the pen and held it in the same way he would drive his knife into a kill. He signed above the line at the bottom of the paper in one quick motion.

"There. Now turn my power back on so my family doesn't freeze to death," Kǫ̀ said and walked out before he could change his mind.

As soon as he was out of sight, Walters picked up the phone.

"We got another parcel."

CHAPTER 14

Kǫ̀ and Ts'ı agreed on most things but, like Christmas, they hit a brick wall when it came to education. Kǫ̀ wanted to keep Kwe and Įt'ǫ̀a out of school completely and teach them how to live on the land instead of learning how to read and write. "It never did me any good," he said every time the word school was mentioned, but Ts'ı insisted they be taught in a classroom like the other kids their age.

"They need to learn to read and write so that they can be strong in both worlds."

"Sounds like residential school to me," Kǫ̀ said.

"Things are different now." Ts'ı tried to offer reassurance.

At the end of the day, Ts'ı had it her way when they found out that children who didn't go regularly could be taken away from their parents by child services, which was enough for Kǫ̀ to buckle.

Kwe and Įt'ǫ̀a went to the same school, the only school in town. A school that had a mix of children from the peninsula and Coppertown. The racial divide on the bus was clear, and Kwe and Įt'ǫ̀a were picked on from the start. Because he was more reserved than his sister and kept mostly to himself, Kwe got it the worst. The Coppertown kids quickly picked up on how shy he was and saw it as an opportunity to make fun of him.

"Hey beaver teeth, chopped down any trees lately with those things?" One boy would start while dangling his fingers in front of his mouth to make it look like teeth.

"Anyone ever tell you, you look like a muskrat?" another boy would say and laugh.

"No, he just eats them. That's why he's starting to look like one too," they said, sneering.

Kwe did his best to ignore them, but Įt'ǫ̀a would always jump in and stick up for her brother every time, yelling at the mean kids to "shut up" but this only caused her to be picked on too. The children chanted out "mouse face, mouse face" every time she got angry, which only made her angrier to the point that Kwe had to hold her back from trying to attack them until the bus driver would lose his patience and yell out some new profanity none of them had ever heard, later to be used in the schoolyard.

Įt'ǫ̀a and Kwe didn't dare tell their parents what was happening on the bus every day, but Ts'ı knew something was wrong when Kwe came home from school one day with a bruised and swollen eye.

"What happened to you?" she cried, holding his chin to bring his face up to the light.

"Some kids on the bus were joking around, that's all," he said, but she could see right through his cover-up.

The next morning, Ts'ı stood at the bus stop with Kwe and Įt'ǫ̀a. When the bus arrived on time, as usual, she asked, "Can you please keep an eye out for these two? I don't want anyone fighting."

The bus driver just looked her over and laughed as Kwe and Įt'ǫ̀a piled in. "I don't know, and I don't care what goes on back there. I'm just the driver," he said and pulled the lever, shutting the door in her face before driving off.

Ts'ı stood on her tippy toes and waved, trying to see them through the windows as the yellow bus sped away. They were embarrassed by their mother, and it didn't take long for the other children on the bus to call them out for "tattletaling."

That same day Ts'ı was already waiting at the bus stop after school before the bus pulled up. She had left early from work so that she could be home to ask them how their day was. Ts'ı herself had been bullied in school and knew what it felt like to have no one she could turn to for protection, except for Kǫ̀, who she hardly ever saw.

The girls at the mission never did like Ts'ı. Not only did she get bullied by the nuns, but she got it from her peers as well. She never did make friends with the other girls and was always by herself in the schoolyard.

As Ts'ı waited for the bus to come around the corner, she saw something light coloured come out of the ditch at the end of the road. Animals had been coming into town more and more with the smell of human food wafting through the air, tempting them to an easy meal. It was mostly bears and foxes that came too close to town, so when Ts'ı saw the distinct pointed furry ears and spotted markings of a lynx, she tried not to startle it. She had never seen a lynx before, but she knew what it was when she saw its clubbed paws that matched the tracks Kǫ̀ once pointed out, explaining that they kept to themselves and usually only hunted at night.

The lynx wasn't alone. She had a small litter. It looked to Ts'ı that the lynx was trying to get her cubs safely across the road, but no sooner had she seen them appear did the school bus came zipping around the corner. The mother heard the bus engine and panicked, bolting to the other side of the road and leaving her babies to fend for themselves. Not wanting the kittens to follow their mother and get run over, Ts'ı made a run for the babies, who were by then wobbling on the side of the road looking lost and crying for their mother their eyes half open. Not knowing what else to do she scooped them up in her arms.

When the bus drove past, Ts'ı put the kittens down beside a prickle bush in the ditch. Confused and whimpering, they didn't move. Ts'ı didn't want to scare the mother off, so she slowly walked away from them as they bobbed their heads.

As soon as she was a good distance away, Ts'ı saw the mom peer out from the bushes. She looked at Ts'ı intensely with her green cat eyes. The mother cat walked back across the street and picked up one of the kittens by the neck and pushed the other one into a roll with her thick furry paw until they disappeared into the thorn brush and found their way back out of town.

The bus was long gone by the time Ts'ı got back to the house and Kwe and Įt'ǫ̀a were already inside.

"Hi Mom, you're home early," Įt'ǫ̀a said.

"Why do you have leaves in your hair?" Kwe asked.

"Well funny story, I just saved two baby lynx from getting run over in the road."

"Sure Mom," Kwe said.

"You mean nǫ̀da."

"What's that?"

"That's what Mamia calls a lynx."

"Right yes nǫ̀da. That's good, Įt'ǫ̀a."

"We should go over and visit Mamia soon, bring her some of her favourite goodies," Ts'ı added.

"Well funny story," Kwe said copying his mother's own words.

"Oh? What's that?"

"You're not supposed to tell," Įt'ǫ̀a blurted out.

"Not supposed to tell me what?" Ts'ı was starting to get worried. "Did one of the kids hurt you again?"

"No," Kwe said.

"We saw Mamia today," Įt'ǫ̀a confessed.

"Mamia? Where? Mamia was at the school?" Ts'ı was confused.

"No, we went to see her at the old folks home," Kwe said.

"During school hours?"

They both nodded their heads knowing they were going to be in trouble.

"Why didn't you tell me you wanted to go see Mamia?"

"Because you're always too busy," Kwe said, it being his idea to skip out on school.

"We miss Mamia," they both said at the same time.

"We never get to see her anymore," Įt'ǫ̀a said sadly.

"Yeah. Whenever we go there, we only get to see her for a few minutes then leave," Įt'ǫ̀a cried.

"So you spent the whole day with her?"

They both looked up at their mother with their big brown eyes and nodded their heads. "She tells us stories. Today she told us about the lynx family," Kwe said.

It's just a coincidence, Ts'ı thought. "Well, I guess that's good that you visited Mamia but you shouldn't be missing school and you need to tell me where you are. Tomorrow when you get on that bus you go to school, you don't get off. You hear me?"

"Okay, Mom," they both agreed.

Ts'ı couldn't fault them for wanting to see Mamia. It was true. They hadn't seen or spoken to her in weeks. How they managed to walk all the way there and back was impressive to Kǫ̀ when Ts'ı told him what they had done and he was glad they went to go see Mamia.

"Mamia's more important than school. School can wait."

After the incident at school, Ts'ı switched shifts with one of the other women who didn't have any children and was able to be home every day before school got out. She would wait for the school bus to make sure Kwe and Įt'ǫ̀a weren't being bothered by the other children but to also make sure they weren't skipping out on school.

Just when Ts'ı thought that the bullying had stopped, one day after school Kwe got off the bus and she noticed he had a fresh red mark on his cheek in the shape of a handprint and a blob of spit in his disheveled hair.

With her adrenaline rushing, Ts'ı jumped onto the bus and pushed past the driver, who yelled, "Hey what are you doing?"

"Which one of you hit my son?" she squinted at the tops of heads in rows as the children sunk down deep into their seats to hide from her. There was a long silence followed by a few snickers.

"That's what I thought. Now leave him alone," she said loudly in her most serious voice, not one to ever lose her temper.

Ts'ı got off the bus in such a way that the driver shut the door slowly behind her this time instead of slamming it like he usually did.

"You're just making it worse," Kwe said under his breath as the bus's brakes released.

"Oh?"

"We can handle it. It's just mostly name calling," Kwe said with an eye roll.

"Yeah. I'm a mouse face," Įt'ǫ̀a said with a skip.

"They call you mouse face?" Ts'ı said, bending down to Įt'ǫ̀a's level.

Įt'ǫ̀a stopped and nodded, waiting to see what her mom was going to say next.

"Come to think of it, yeah you do look like a little mouse," she said, pinching her nose, and they all walked up the steep steps to the house with their heads held high not letting the bullies get the best of them.

CHAPTER 15

Kǫ did not come from a wealthy family, but he knew what it felt like to be rich. A different kind of rich. A wealth that could only be found when out on the land. Yet without money he no longer had the freedom to go out on the land. He had his canoe but most people had boat engines and since he no longer had a dog team he wasn't able to travel very far in winter unless he borrowed a skidoo. Eventually, he managed to save some of the money he made from working in the gold mine to buy his own skidoo. He could get back on the land again and maybe even build the cabin he dreamed of.

The place he had in mind was the only place that felt right. Ts'ı's birthplace. It was there that he swore he would one day build their cabin. He and Kwe would build it together. The vision of a home in the bush was all he needed to hold on to so he could get through the dark and dreary days, but just when Kǫ was finally able to save up enough money for his dream to come true, a notice was slipped under his door.

When Kǫ heard the faint knock, he opened the door only to see a vehicle with government licence plates speed away. The bold letters on the paper gave him a headache when he tried to make any sense of them, so he waited for Kwe to come home from school to read it out loud.

"Go ahead, read it out," Kǫ said to Kwe with his arms crossed and his feet shoulder-width apart at the ready for what could only be bad news.

Kwe picked up the paper and read it aloud.

"The Housing Corporation has increased the monthly rent based on your annual income as per Policy 13.1 of the housing rental rating scale. We have recently reviewed your income report from last year and you have earned over the amount allowable for our low-income supplement program. If you do not comply with this notice and pay the increase you will be given an eviction warning. You have until ..."

Kwe would have kept reading but Kǫ̀ stopped him. "Enough. Give it here." Kǫ̀ took back the paper and walked out of the kitchen, regretting that he brought his son into it.

It was the end of the day on a Friday heading into the long weekend when Kǫ̀ barged into the housing office and slammed the crumpled paper on Walters' desk, causing Nora to jump up and chase after him.

"Mr. Collins, you need an appointment."

"My name's not Collins." He shot a dart at her with his eyes.

"It's okay, Nora. I've got this," Walters said, getting to his feet and yanking up his pants at the front in a constant losing battle with his belt.

"What can I help you with now, Christian?" he said, trying to make himself look larger than he already was inside of his musty office.

"It's just one thing after another with you, isn't it? First, you take the land, then you try to tear my family apart and now you're trying to take away the last of my hard-earned money?"

"You got the letter, I presume," Walters said gruffly like he just drank a big glass of milk. "Listen, like I said before, I'm not in the business of putting people out, but you signed the paper. There's nothing more I can do to help you."

"No, it's not the way it is. You're not getting another red cent from me. This paper means nothing." Kǫ̀ took the paper back and stormed out the door feeling a slight flicker of liberation deep down in his gut, but the feeling was soon muted by the thought of what might happen if he didn't pay.

When he got home, Kǫ̀ couldn't bring himself to tell Ts'ı about his encounter with Walters. He kept quiet and half expected the housing office to come knocking at any moment to tell them they were being evicted for not paying but nothing happened.

Kǫ̀ kept his word and stopped paying the housing office, hoping it would be forgotten and the housing debts climbed. Then Ts'ı came home one day from work one day to see an eviction notice under the door.

"What's this?" she asked as he walked into the house from work.

"Can I take my boots off first?" He swore under his breath, not at her but at himself for not being honest with her. When he sat down at the table, she looked down at him waiting for an answer.

"I'm not paying it," he said stubbornly without looking her in the eyes.

"What do you mean? How long has this been going on?" The pitch in her voice rising in learning that he had kept something hidden from her.

"Since the summer."

She suddenly needed to sit down.

"Since the summer? Kǫ̀, what are you thinking? We're going to get evicted," she whispered weak with despair and put her head in her hands.

"No, we're not. They can't do that to us. Woods hasn't paid his rent in how long and he's bootlegging on top of it. I don't see anyone doing anything about that." He pointed in the direction of Woods's house.

“That’s his problem, Kǫ̀, not ours. Our bills are piled to the roof. We owe so much money!” she cried.

“That’s just it. Don’t you see? We don’t owe them anything. They owe us. They’re the ones who tore our house apart, our family.” Kǫ̀ stood up and looked out the kitchen window hoping she would see things his way for once.

“Just please, Kǫ̀, start paying it. It’s the dead of winter. We can’t be left in the cold again.” She rose to her feet to meet him.

“Why don’t you go buy more of those tickets then, huh? Maybe that’ll get us out of this rut. We can’t ever win, T’si. We won’t ever win. They won’t let us,” Kǫ̀ said.

“Stop it, Kǫ̀. Its not true.”

“It’s true, Ts’ı. Its all the same, don’t you see. Nobody wins except them,” he said slapping the eviction notice paper. “Actually, no. You know what? Maybe I’m wrong. Maybe you will win. You know why, Ts’ı? Cause you’re turning into one of them,” he said accusingly and walked out the door.

“Don’t say that, Kǫ̀. Don’t you ever say that!” she cried after him.

Kǫ̀ had never talked to Ts’ı that way in all the time they had been together, and he blamed it all on the house. How senseless, he thought, to blame his outbursts on a house. What had he become? He was growing more and more resentful as each moment passed, losing himself in the midst of it all.

He was angry at Walters, angry at his brother, angry at the kids and now Ts’ı. He couldn’t control himself. He needed an outlet.

Kǫ̀ had never drunk a drop of alcohol in his life but that night was the first time it crossed his mind to have a drink to help take his worries away, if only for a night.

Would it really be so bad, he thought? It was a Saturday afternoon — the day designated for taking a break from work, but Kǫ̀ never fell for such a farce. Every day there was something to do when he was a child. Now he didn’t know what to do with himself on his days off.

As he walked in the misty snowfall lit up under the streetlights, he passed the busy row of bars, where the smell of stale beer and loud country music drifted out onto the street. Where every night a rowdy bar fight broke out. He thought about going inside but what would Ts'ı think if she found him there? What would the kids think? Thoughts of his family's disappointment changed his mind. He needed to be strong for them; they counted on him, relied on him. The bar was the last place Ts'ı would ever expect him to be, and he wanted to keep it that way.

He thought about checking his traps but it was still too early; he had just put them out that morning. It was his father who had shown him how to set traps, how to loop the snare and tie it low around a tree. Kǫ̀ remembered how upset he was about not catching anything in his trapline the first time he checked in anticipation.

"*Asìı mǫhdaà gonìk'è agot'ı̨-le hò ats'ǫ naxìnà dahwhǫ. Ats'ǫ mahsì dahwhǫ. Įlè dahwhǫ-le xè ı̨hwhą dahwhǫ-le.*" His father's words about the importance of being patient and remaining happy at all times were so simple yet so difficult to put into practice then and especially now that he found himself so miserable.

Kǫ̀ walked and walked, wandering aimlessly for hours, not knowing which way to go, but when he finally stopped and looked up, he found himself right where he needed to be, in front of the old folks home.

He hadn't seen his mother in some time. Their daily visits turned weekly, then monthly. He knew the kids went to see her often and didn't think she would care to see him as much. Besides, his job had him too busy but now that he was standing in front of her window, he couldn't remember the last time he had seen her.

My poor mother, he thought. Alone in this place. Had Woods even gone to visit her?

Kǫ̀ looked at the octagon-shaped building in front of him. It was late and the motion lights flickered on when he walked past, lighting up the night in a soft yellow. He could see that the ramp leading up to the doorway needed a good shovel.

Through the front door window he saw the nurses at a table in the main room playing cards. She wouldn't want to see me in such a state. I'll visit her tomorrow. Visiting hours are over, he told himself as an excuse, but when the light from a small lamp turned on in one of the units above him and the shadow of her small frame moved across the room to the window, she smiled and waved him in.

"It's late, Mamia. I hope I didn't wake you," Kǫ̀ said as he stepped into her room and pulled up a chair next to her bed.

"It's okay. I don't sleep much these days anyways," she said, sitting down next to her mountain of pillows.

"How did you know I was outside?"

"A mother knows," she said, smiling with her eyes. "Have a mint." She pointed at a clear bowl on her nightstand.

"No, thanks."

"You're not supposed to say no when someone offers you something, you know that," she said lightly, grabbing a small handful and tapping his hand so he would open it up and take some.

"They're always filling up my candy dish around here. You'd think I had teeth. These things are so hard. I never eat them. Just give them away to my visitors, Kwe and Įt'ǫ̀a." She smiled with a twinkle in her eyes reserved for her grandchildren.

Kǫ̀ looked over at the full candy dish and felt sorry he hadn't visited sooner.

"How's my grandbabies?" she asked. "I miss them."

"They're good. Have they been visiting?"

"They come when they can. I know they are busy with their friends and their school."

"Well I know they miss you too."

"Last time I saw them, it was Įt'ǫ̀a's birthday. She's so big now," she said, then paused not wanting to make him feel sorry for her.

"I don't mind it here. Your father's brother is here. Did you know that? Your uncle Bayha. You remember him, don't you? We sometimes visit and talk about the way things used to be."

"I wish I did. I hardly even remember my father anymore," Kǫ̀ said and they both no longer knew what to say.

Kǫ̀ broke through the silence by changing the subject. "They switched me onto the processor at the mine. It's a bit more money."

"I know. People talk. But you're not happy about it, are you?" she said.

"It pays the bills." He shrugged.

"You need to get back to what you love, Kǫ̀," she said, worried.

"How can I when what I love always seems to be taken from me."

"Kǫ̀, what you love can never truly be taken away."

Kǫ̀ wanted to ask what she meant. He wanted so badly for her to give him the answer to solving his problems, but they were interrupted by a knock on the door.

"How'd you get in here? Visiting hours are over."

"Just give us a bit please," Kǫ̀ said hoping that good manners might work in his favour.

Mamia interjected, "That's alright, I'm getting tired anyway, my dear. Tell Ts'ı and the kids I love them?"

He leaned in to hug her and she kissed him on the cheek.

"Kǫ̀ …" she said as he reached over to turn the lamp off for her.

"Yes."

"Keep it on please. I like the light."

"Ok neghǫnehtǫ, toò nezı̨ whenetı̨." The words were still hard for Kǫ̀ to say out loud but he practised telling her he loved her whenever he got the chance.

"Sı̨ sı̀ı neghǫnehtǫ, Kǫ̀. Don't worry, your heart will find its way home again."

CHAPTER 16

As the years went by, Kộ never called in sick to work. Never missing a day, he would have worked seven days a week if he could, but like Saturday, Sunday was also a day off. Sunday, however, was the day the missionaries devoted to God. The day of rest. So naturally, on that day Kộ did the opposite. He worked harder than ever doing things around the house, helping his neighbours seal drafty doors, fix leaky plumbing, paint over chipped and flaky paint.

Kộ threw himself into his job too. With every shovel that he buried into the ground, every rock face he chiseled looking for gold, every bit of hard labour that he was ordered to do, he did so bitterly for having to exploit the land against his will.

Despite resenting his job, Kộ found work to be fairly easy. He resisted putting his name in at first when the mine recruitment manager offered jobs to most of the men from the peninsula. He wanted to know what exactly he would be getting himself into. He had already checked out the mine on his own, investigating things for himself. He didn't have to climb over the gate that said "Keep Out" to get in as it didn't go around the entire perimeter of the property. He merely walked alongside the fence until it stopped abruptly next to a creek.

It didn't take much for him to wade through the water up to his knees and reach the other side of a small hill where he found a huge hole in the ground half the size of Coppertown itself. It wasn't the only hole in the ground either. As he walked around the giant quarry careful not to get too close to the edge, he spotted more like it in the distance. Large boulders inside the earth walls looked like they were ready to drop at any minute, held uncertainly by dirt and damaged tree roots from where the trees were cut and thrown into brush piles that when burned would turn the colour of a chemical rainbow from the mine's emissions, polluting the grounds and everything around it.

Kǫ̀ tried to stay off the road and out of sight but was spotted by two men who were making the rounds in their work truck.

"Hey, you're not supposed to be in here," the driver yelled out of the open window.

Kǫ̀ picked up his pace walking towards the way he came in.

"Hey man. Are you looking for work?"

Kǫ̀ stopped and slowly turned back around now that he knew they weren't going to mess with him.

"I might be," he lied.

"The head office is that way. You can go sign your name up for a labourer position." The man pointed. "Want a lift?"

"I'm good," Kǫ̀ said and continued walking back towards the creek while the men looked at each other, confused as to where he was going.

The pressure of having to find a way to pay bills was too much for Kǫ̀ and he gave in. No longer could he tinker around and help in the community for free. He had to bring money into the household. With Ts'ı working to make ends meet it was only right that he contribute too, but each minute he spent down in those cramped, dark tunnels surrounded by the oldest rocks in the world, named after his only son, was unsettling. The cold, damp hollow mineshaft only served as a reflection of how he felt inside, and it didn't take long for the conflict to show up in his body. He was sore all the time. Every joint, ligament and bone ached.

Even when he was at home, he couldn't get away from work. From his partially thawed living room window, steamed in condensation from the heat of the woodstove that he illegally installed to lower the costs of the heat bill after their power was shut off, Kǫ̀ had a miserable view of the old wooden mineshaft. Its rickety and decrepit-looking frame stood like a curse across the lake, destroying what was once an uninterrupted view. He could never understand how such an entity, such a force, could do so much damage by human hands. The land had been turned into a moneymaking machine, driven by greed.

In his mind, the mine was a murderer. The manpower behind it gave it its strength, but it seemed to have taken on a life of its own. Kǫ̀ knew that the constant taking could never allow for nature to coexist. The mine was disruptive in every way imaginable, and it could only lead to a place there was no coming back from.

The passage of time proved that Kǫ̀ was right about one thing; the mine was a force so powerful that it set out on a rampage of serial killing that no one could stop. Mine production was not carefully maintained, and the pollution coming out of the smokestacks landing on the banks of creeks began to kill off the animals first.

Workers reported seeing entire schools of fish floating in the creeks, mallards turned up dead, their eggs not able to hatch. An entire family of beavers were found with rigor mortis near a dam. All had the markings of poisoning. Even the scavengers left them alone, sniffing out a sickness that humans couldn't.

With all these findings, still the mine didn't stop production. Mine management turned a blind eye to what was happening to the animals whose habitats happened to be in the vicinity of the mine. It was only when the ravens started dropping from the sky in town that people started to question why.

"Falling from the sky," the front page of the newspaper read with a picture of a dead bird on the ground. It was common to see the odd dead raven next to a power pole, zapped by the electrical current and causing the power all over town to go out but this was different. Mine workers knew that the ravens were eating the leftover lunch they tossed onto the ground behind the cafeteria. The ravens had set up their nests under the ledges of some of the higher buildings like the mineshaft itself for easy access to food scraps.

When the ravens started coming into town, they were sending a message that something wasn't right. Abandoning their nests, they came by the thousands, darkening the sky in the middle of the day with their black wings. They perched on the main government building, making a mess of the siding. It got to be so bad that government workers could no longer work with the constant squawking and janitors were tasked with climbing up ladders to install spikes so that the ravens wouldn't land on the windowsill before falling mysteriously to their death on the sidewalk below.

Next, it was the fish. When Kǫ̀ checked his traps, he was turning up bug-eyed-looking fish in the bay near the mine. Some with only one eye or three gills, some filled with a bright green slime and an overwhelming odour seeping from their stomachs when cut open. Kǫ̀ brought one home to show Ts'ı after turning up more than one.

"I think we should report this."

"I've tried. They won't listen," Kǫ̀ said.

"People are going to get sick if they eat this," she said as she held her nose closed from the stench of the deformed fish laid out on the table in front of her on a black garbage bag.

"I'm throwing it back. One of the kwet'ı̨ı̀ from town's bound to report it. From now on, we don't eat fish until we figure out what's going on."

"Do you think …" Ts'ı didn't want to say it but she looked out at the mine in accusation.

"I don't know what to think anymore. I sure as hell hope not but what else could it be?"

"If it is, do you think they'll shut it down?"

"Not a chance."

As Kǫ̀ suspected, soon the local fishermen and restaurant owners stopped fishing altogether in the parts of the lake adjacent to the mine and reported the sickly looking fish to the government, who had, around the same time, established their own fisheries complaint department.

It was more than mere speculation by that point that the mine was causing abnormalities in the fish nearby. People in town were certain that the mine had a direct link to not only the fish but all the small water-dwelling animals that were turning up dead or severely sick, but no one wanted to admit it. After all, most of the townspeople would be out of a job if the mine were to shut down and they weren't going to let anything come between them and their livelihood, not the land, the water, the animals, not even their own lives.

The mine not only continued without skipping a beat but it also advanced its agenda going full force into production, and the health of the land, water and animals fell further into decline. Kǫ̀ continued working, at war with himself about why he couldn't just quit. Every day he came home with the same complaint. "It's that damn mine, and everybody knows it. They're just not admitting it. Next, it's gonna be the people, you just watch."

Ts'ı just shook her had sadly as she plated their dinner.

"Did you tell the kids to stop going near the bank of the water by the bay? Tell them they can't even go near it," Kǫ̀ said urgently after hearing some other workers saying the lake could very well be contaminated with arsenic.

"They haven't been down there in a long time. They don't swim there anymore." Kǫ̀ wouldn't have known. Having worked so much he didn't notice how much older the kids were getting.

"When I was young, I'd jump off those rocks and swim all

day. Seems like another lifetime ago now." Ts'ı looked at him in surprise to hear him talk about his childhood, something he rarely spoke about.

"The lake's right outside our door for Christ's sakes. What's it gonna be next?"

"Noreen's brother drew their drinking water from the bay a few days ago and the entire family's been sick since," Ts'ı said sadly as she stirred her food around on her plate, having lost her appetite.

Kǫ̀ couldn't live in denial anymore. He had to say what had been playing on his mind for some time. He hung his head and banged his hand on the table. "What if that's how Į̨t'ǫ̀a got sick?" Kǫ̀ belted. "It had to have been. She got sick around the same time the mine was going into production. What else could it be? Come to think of it, they were having trouble with one of the stacks from the start." Kǫ̀ stared at Ts'ı wide eyed, the veil lifting as he said out loud what he had subconsciously feared all that time.

"I had a hand in it Ts'ı. I almost killed our daughter." Kǫ̀ gritted his teeth and brought his clenched fist to his forehead to stop himself from crying.

Ts'ı got up and moved around to his side of the table to comfort him with her hand on his shoulder. "You couldn't have. How could you have known. There's no way. She's okay now. It's not your fault."

"That's it, I'm gonna quit." It wasn't the first time he had uttered the threat. He paused when he noticed that Ts'ı seemed to be elsewhere.

Any other time, he wouldn't have noticed the solemn look in her eyes but when he saw her reflection in the window looking past the old encased rotted wood and patches of black mould, Kǫ̀ knew something wasn't right.

"What is it?" Kǫ̀ asked.

Ts'ı switched her gaze onto him.

"Your mother, she's not doing so well. The kids and I went to see her yesterday. She could hardly get up on her own. I didn't want to tell you. You've got enough to worry about."

"I just went to see her not too long ago. She seemed okay," he said puzzled.

Ts'ı just shook her head sadly.

"You'd better go see her." It wasn't the news that Ts'ı wanted to bring, but Mamia had taken a turn for the worst.

CHAPTER 17

A smile hid the pain when Kǫ̀ walked into her room. Seeing her jar of mints still full filled him with pity. He went to her bedside and held her hand.

"Mamia, how are you?" he asked softly.

"Oh I fell, Kǫ̀. I was trying to get some fresh air, and I slid down the ramp and landed on my good side," she said. "I've been having some pain. I didn't want you to worry."

"Why didn't you tell me?" Kǫ̀ cried.

"I'm okay. Really." She patted his hand.

Kǫ̀ helped her into a sitting position and propped up a few pillows behind her back to help her hold up the warm bowl of chicken noodle soup the worker brought in for her dinner.

"I sure do miss cooking," she said.

"How is it?"

"You try it and tell me what you think." He tried a sip and made a sour face.

"Some fresh bannock might help make it taste better." She laughed.

"How 'bout I make you your favourite, rabbit stew. None of this fake canned stuff," he said trying to cheer her up. Just then the starting night shift worker came in the room to usher him out.

"Visiting hours are over."

"Just a few more minutes," Kǫ̀'s mother asked, and the worker disapprovingly left the room.

"Bring me that blanket, will you Kǫ̀? It's cold."

As Kộ covered her with the blanket and tucked it in around her, it was then that she said, "I think you're ready to know about what happened to your father."

Kộ was taken aback. He would never be ready but prepared himself for what she was about to say.

"Your father … he fought back."

"What do you mean?"

"When he found out they took you, he caught up to one of the boats in his canoe when one of them stopped on shore to pick up more children, thinking you were in it."

As she spoke, Kộ's mind flashed back to the sounds of the bells. Searching his memory, Kộ suddenly saw his father fighting off two large men in red a short distance from where he floated.

A loud ringing went off in Kộ's ears when he remembered the sound of the gunshots. All his life it was far safer for Kộ to believe his father had left his own family than to accept his murder. Blocking it from his memory was all he could do to shield his heart from breaking.

"He never survived. He wasn't going to let you go …" She stopped, unable to go on.

Kộ felt a sharp pain in his chest knowing his father sacrificed his own life to try and save him. As much as the truth was devasting to hear, at the same time, the heavy weight of a lifetime of built-up resentment towards his father fell away instantly and was replaced with an overwhelming respect for the man he always knew his father to be.

There was nothing left for either of them to say. What was done was done. Kộ held his mother's hand and sat next to her bedside until she fell asleep. On his way out, he looked over at the ramp that his mother fell down to see that the workers still hadn't even cleared the snow.

Kộ looked around for a shovel and happened to see one leaning against the building on the other side of the steps. He grabbed it and began shoveling madly. Shoveling away the pain and anger that had burdened his family for a lifetime. He chipped away at the hardened chunks of ice under the snow piercing each piece with the pointed edge of the metal shovel until the thin ice broke in half and he was able to scrape it off, long slivers of wood coming off with it.

The scraping of metal on wood made such a loud sound it woke Mamia. Using all her strength, she got up slowly and shuffled her way to the window to have one last look at her grown son. He looked back at her as cold gusts of air hovered in a mist above his head and gave a short wave. She waved back. Kǫ̀ put his head down and continued shoveling, unaware that it would be their last goodbye.

The next morning, Kǫ̀ was already back from checking his traps before the sun came up. He was surprised to see that almost every one of his wire traps had a white rabbit caught in it. Even in the year after the government declared a wolf cull because too many wolves were coming into town, it was the most rabbits he had ever harvested at one time.

Kǫ̀ skinned one of the rabbits and before anyone was awake, he was already stirring the stew he promised to deliver to Mamia when he got the call.

"Hello?"

"Mr. Collins?"

"Who's this?"

"Mr. Collins. I'm sorry to tell you that your mother died in her sleep last night." The director of the old folks home broke the news almost robotically, having delivered the message hundreds of times before.

"You must have her mixed up with someone else. I was just with her last night and she was fine."

"I'm sorry for your loss. These kinds of things are hard to

accept. We'll need you to come down and sign papers to get started on the funeral arrangements," the woman said and hung up. Kǫ̀ continued to stir his soup in denial.

Ts'ı and the kids were still asleep when he filled his work thermos with warm stew and walked it over to Mamia at the old folks home. But when he walked into her bedroom it was empty, the jar of stale mints gone, moved to another room, given to another Elder.

"Where is she?" He demanded to know where they moved her when the worker that kicked him out the night before popped her head into the empty room after hearing his wet squeaky footsteps from his rubber boots enter the building from down the hall.

"Come with me," she said.

She led him to where they moved Mamia's body — where she lay covered in a white sheet in one of the back rooms until they could transport her to the morgue.

Kǫ̀ shook his head. "No, it can't be." But when he walked over to her and slowly lifted the sheet that covered her colourless face, he went numb. Mamia's eyes were closed, her chest sunken, her spirit gone.

"She wasn't supposed to die yet. She'd still be alive if she were home," Kǫ̀ cried. "She'd still be alive," he said out loud mostly to himself as he hung his head in misery at her side, wishing he had more time with her.

"I know this is hard. I'll give you some time alone," the caregiver said and left the room.

He stood for a long time by her side holding her hand. For the first time, he noticed the lines on her face, the wrinkles at the corners of her eyes, the wiry grey hairs that framed her face. She had been through so much in her lifetime, seen so many changes.

He brushed away his tears knowing she wouldn't want him to be sad. There was no sense in him lingering any longer. She was no longer with him. He leaned in and kissed her on the cheek and walked out without looking back. He took his time walking back home carrying the steel container filled with warm rabbit stew, unsure of how he was going to give his family the news.

Kǫ̀ made sure that his mother would have a traditional ceremony. He vaguely remembered seeing one of his uncles being buried as a child. They had placed him in a cradled position so that his body would return to the earth in the same way it is carried in the womb before being brought into the world.

Kǫ̀ made his mother's casket by hand, and together Ts'ı, Kwe and Įt'ǫ̀a helped bring her body back out onto the land to lay her to rest. Woods managed to stay sober long enough to attend his mother's send-off. He built her a crooked cross out of treated plywood to put on her burial site, but Kǫ̀ wouldn't allow it.

Back at the house, Kǫ̀ tried to muster the memories of the times with her that he did have but he could hardly see past the damp, decaying walls of his own heart, a heart that now mirrored the house he was bound by. His sadness had no home.

On the eve of Mamia's burial, he dreamt of the time they all went on their first hunting trip together. In his dream, he returned to the waterfall where he and Kwe saw the muskox, but when it went to climb up the rocks next to the falls, it lost its footing and large boulders gave way underneath, causing the animal to go down with the crumbling cliff, crashing violently into the rushing water and disappearing into the rapids below.

He woke up in his dream to hear someone shuffling outside of his tent. It was the Indian agent with pen and paper in hand. Kǫ̀ tried to speak, to tell him to go away, but no words came out, even when he tried to yell at the top of his lungs.

CHAPTER 18

A few years later, Kwe's new bright yellow bike was taken from the side of the house in broad daylight. The peninsula became a place where you had to lock your doors, and Kwe's bike being stolen was just the start of it.

The kid from down the road brazenly rode it home and spray painted it white, only to throw it in a pile with the other stolen bikes he collected behind a tall fence with an unchained guard dog.

Telling his son he had to guard his belongings against theft wasn't a lesson that Kǫ̀ wanted to teach. To Kǫ̀, community was supposed to be a place of trust and support, not a place where you had to always watch your back. Yet it wasn't the petty theft that Kǫ̀ was overly concerned about. He was worried about bigger problems on the rise.

Kǫ̀ soon became aware of the illegal activities that were taking place on the peninsula. Just as bad if not worse than his brother, the drug dealers usually came out at night when everyone was asleep.

The dealers drove slowly past houses when all the lights were off trying to be inconspicuous by driving just under the speed limit, but Kǫ̀ could hear the humming of the car engines and the sound of tires on gravel and knew that they were up to no good and he wasn't the only one.

At a community meeting, Chief and Council were asked to do something about the growing drug problem but the leaders just batted away the complaints. "We can't do anything if we don't have evidence."

Despite the few who were not afraid to expose the criminals, most people in the community turned a blind eye to the drug dealers out of fear that they might face retaliation if they told what they knew. Then there were those who were directly related to the drug dealers involved in the gangs from the south. Even the Elders resorted to drug dealing to make ends meet. To pay their housing debts. Whatever it took not to have to live in shambles. They used the money to buy food for their grandchildren while their parents indulged in an ever-growing drug problem that was circling the community.

To try and deal with the drug problem and appease the regular complainers, Chief and Council made an ice rink on the lake for the youth to help keep them out of trouble. Kwe was one of the first to try it out, keen on learning how to skate.

"Are you sure it's free?"

"Yeah, Dad."

Nothing was free anymore to Kǫ̀. "There's got to be a catch."

"No, Dad, they even have skates and sticks for us."

"What do you think, Mom?" Kǫ̀ asked.

"Sure, why not. It might be fun," Ts'ı said.

Although the skates weren't sharpened and the sticks were a choice between cheap wood or itchy fibreglass, Kǫ̀ noticed quickly that Kwe had a knack for skating. He could glide easily across the jagged ice. He could get past most of the kids effortlessly, even the ones who were bigger than him, and he scored a goal within the first few minutes of putting on his skates. Soon he became so good that he wanted to try playing on an actual team.

"Dad, can you put me in real hockey?"

"Like on a team?"

"Yeah ..." said Kwe.

"I don't know. You better ask Mom."

Ts'ı wasn't sure it was such a good idea. "I don't know Kǫ̀. I don't want him to get hurt."

"Look at him. He's a natural," Kǫ̀ said. "He needs to get out of the house anyway and away from that tv."

"I guess," she said reluctantly, more worried about how he would fit in on a team made up of Coppertown kids.

Once Kwe was officially enrolled in the Coppertown hockey league, he tried not to let it bother him that he was the only kid representing the peninsula and the only player with a different colour skin than the rest of them. When he laced up his skates and set his sights on the puck, it was apparent to everyone that he didn't only stand out because he was not one of them because he skated circles around every other player on the team.

It would have been nice for him to be lifted up by the other players and cheered on, but even those on his own team soon became jealous of his strengths on the ice, and it didn't take long for them to start in on him. Whenever one of the players would catch up to him on the ice, they would slam him hard into the boards and taunt him. Most of them, having known him since grade school, jumped in, and before he knew it, he was back to being called "muskrat," making it impossible for him to ignore. Even the referees and coaches turned a blind eye to the unfair players who took turns taking cheap shots at Kwe.

In the locker room after each game, Kwe was an easy target. It got so bad that Kwe made sure to be the first one off the ice and out of the rink. He wasn't like them and never would be. But he wished he was so that he could at least fit in for once.

Regardless, Kwe never gave up. He loved the game too much. He played his first tournament against a few of the hometown teams and all but won single-handedly by scoring a hat trick but that didn't change the way he was treated. After the game, when it came time for everyone to shake hands, the other team wouldn't even look at Kwe. Even the coaches didn't extend a hand or a pat on the back.

"What's going on out there?" Kǫ̀ asked when he saw that his son wasn't being treated with the celebration he deserved for nearly winning the game. Kǫ̀ had been so busy working hard to afford to keep his son in hockey that he had difficulty finding the time to watch his games and couldn't see for himself how unfairly Kwe was being treated.

"It's nothing. Let's go," Kwe said, with his head hung low, walking ahead of his dad and out of the rink.

"What was that out there, Muskrat? You tryin' to show us up?" the captain of the team said as he shoved Kwe into a sitting position on the bench in the locker room after another one of his best games.

The other teammates continued to unlace their skates, most of them carelessly snickering under their breath. As the teasing went on, only a few of them wanted to stand up to the captain and tell him to back off but didn't dare in case they too got bullied.

Kwe already had his gear off and was ready to leave. He got back up and walked past the captain without a word, trying to avoid a confrontation but before he could reach the door the captain yelled, "Hey Muskrat, catch." And he spun a spare puck like a frisbee in Kwe's direction at eye level.

Kwe didn't turn around, and it was a good thing or he would have lost an eye. The puck hit him in the back of the head, slicing clean through his flesh to the bone. He didn't drop to the ground, didn't even put his hand on his head. He only stopped for a moment as everyone stayed stark silent waiting to see what was going to happen next, some expecting he would turn around and fight back. Instead, Kwe continued to walk out the door.

The coach was on his way into the locker room as Kwe was on his way out. He saw the dazed look in Kwe's eyes but didn't bother to offer up a "good game son." Not even a "well done" or a pat on the back was given for his amazing performance on the ice. All that was said was, "You got lucky." In a less than impressive tone, not noticing the blood from Kwe's head starting to run a steady stream down his neck.

"Uh huh," were all the words that Kwe could put together.

On his way to the truck, Kwe grabbed a towel from his bag and held it up to his head, pretending to wipe the sweat from his hair before getting in next to his mom, who had to move into the middle of the bucket seat to make room.

"Good game son. I'm proud of you." Kǫ̀ didn't notice how pale Kwe was but Ts'ı did right away.

"Are you alright?" Ts'ı asked. "Why are you holding your head like that?"

Kwe didn't answer; he just stared straight ahead.

"Kǫ̀, look at him. Something's wrong," Ts'ı said, nudging Kǫ̀ with her elbow.

"What's the matter, Kwe?" Kǫ̀ reached over from the driver's side and pulled Kwe's hand away to see the large gash in his head. The blood made his thick black hair shine around the wound all matted and sticky.

"What happened?" Kǫ̀ yelled. "You're bleeding!"

But still, Kwe didn't answer.

Kǫ̀ sped straight to the hospital as Kwe slowly closed his eyes and bobbed his head every time his dad hit a pothole.

After his head was all sewn up, the doctor told Kǫ̀ and Ts'ı that Kwe had a severe concussion and needed to take a break from hockey. His hair around the scar would never grow back.

Hockey became out of the question for Kwe. Ts'ı just wouldn't allow it, and Kwe began to act out of character because of it. He had changed from a quiet reserved kid to a restless and bored teenager. No longer able to do what he loved, with so much free time on his hands from no longer playing hockey, he started hanging around town and skipping school. That's when he met Nelson. Kwe had always known who Nelson was because, like him, he was also from the peninsula but they never hung out. In fact, it was Nelson who had stolen Kwe's bike.

Nelson was a troubled kid. His father had left his mother when he was young, and she had a hard time looking after him on her own. He was in and out of foster homes and always getting into trouble with the law. Nelson had no discipline, giving him the freedom to do anything he pleased. He never did go to school and was often caught drinking and doing drugs on the rocks behind the school.

Kwe wasn't allowed to hang out with Nelson, but since the assault, Kwe didn't care if he got into trouble. All his inhibitions were gone, and he began to care less and less about what his parents wanted for him.

When Kwe didn't come home one day after school, Ts'ı was so worried that she asked Kǫ to go out and look for him the second he came in the door from working overtime.

Kǫ dropped his bag in the doorway. Without taking his work boots off he turned back around to go looking for Kwe, knowing it wasn't like him to stay out so late even though he had been testing his parents more and more.

Kǫ spent the night driving around the community looking for Kwe, going to all the usual spots where the local teenagers hung out, but Kwe was nowhere to be found.

A few months before Kwe's hockey incident, Kǫ had given in and bought a used truck. He didn't want to admit it, but he appreciated having the ability to get around much quicker, that and being able to drive Kwe to and from the rink. Even if it wasn't the same as running his old dog team, Kǫ was glad that he didn't have to rely on a ride to work each day from one of his less than reliable co-workers.

Kǫ̀ had a feeling to turn off the highway and onto a back road that led to both a cemetery and a large open pit that was used as a sliding hill in the winter. Sure enough, Kǫ̀ saw the glimmer of red brake lights through the trees at the turn into the open pit. As Kǫ̀ slowly drove up, he thought the truck might have been stuck in the mud but when he got closer, he noticed the truck was full of smoke. He could barely make out the faces inside but knew that it had to be Kwe because of the loud rock music blaring out of it nearly busting the speakers, the same music that Kwe resorted to playing on repeat in his bedroom to drown out the world.

Kwe was laughing and joking with his friends until he happened to look out the window after seeing something moving out of the corner of his eye in the rear-view mirror. The figure was walking quickly towards them out of the old cemetery. Kwe thought he was seeing things at first and said, suddenly frightened, "Yo, is that a person?"

"Ha, ha you're just trippin'." Nelson laughed. "Objects in mirror are closer than they appear."

"No, seriously guys … I think it's my … my dad!" Kwe said in shock as he peered through the window to see his dad's upset expression meet him at eye level.

"Holy shit, it is your dad," Nelson said.

"Drive, man. Drive!" one of the kids yelled from the back seat and the driver, whose parents the vehicle belonged to, stepped on the gas without thinking and sped off, driving over Kǫ̀'s foot.

"You want to tell me what you were doing in the cemetery tonight, son?" Kǫ̀ asked as he shuffled to find a comfortable position on the faded flower-print couch they'd had since they moved in, adjusting the ice pack on his foot.

"What do you mean?" Kwe asked dully.

"Don't lie to me!" Kǫ̀ yelled, accidently waking up Įt'ǫ̀a.

"You're home," Ts'ı said in relief, appearing from the kitchen in her robe after putting on the tea.

"You want to explain to your mother what you were doing in the cemetery tonight?"

"I wasn't even at the cemetery. I was at Nelson's," he said and walked to his room, slamming the door boldly behind him, knowing his dad was not in the best shape to get up and follow him to scold him.

Įt'ǫ̀a came out of her room to see what the commotion was and sat beside her dad, rubbing her eyes. "What happened to your foot?"

"Nothing. I'm okay. Don't worry about your old dad," he lied and she rested her head on his shoulder.

After that, Kǫ̀ caught Kwe more often than not coming home late on the weekends, drunk and high. Kǫ̀ and Ts'ı were at a loss about what to do. They tried disciplining Kwe by taking away the things he loved but he didn't care. He lost interest in most things, and depriving him only served to make him rebel even more. The only thing they could do was ground him and for a day or two it worked, but one night Kǫ̀ woke up with the sense that something wasn't quite right. Come to think of it, he thought it unusual that Kwe had gone to bed early that evening and was overly polite, but by the same token, he was happy to see his son finally in a good mood.

Only when Kǫ̀ walked into the dark kitchen to grab a glass of water in the middle of the night did he happen to see out the window by the light of the moon that his truck was gone.

As it was, Kộ wasn't used to seeing a vehicle parked in the driveway and almost went back to bed still groggy but when he fully came to, he could see that his truck was indeed gone. He tossed his water into the sink and slammed the cup down on the counter.

Kộ walked over to where he kept the keys to his truck, in the top front pocket of his work overalls hanging by the front door, to make sure he wasn't dreaming. Sure enough, they were gone. Kộ was livid. He never would have pulled such a stunt in all his life. It had him questioning where he went wrong as he walked into Kwe's room, already knowing he wasn't going to find his son asleep in his bed. He ripped off the covers of the mattress to see that Kwe had placed his pillows to make it look like he was asleep as he had seen in his tv shows.

"Ts'ı!" Kộ flicked on the light switch in their bedroom in a mad rush.

"He took my truck," Kộ said as he fumbled and tripped trying to get his pants on in a hurry.

Ts'ı sat up in bed trying to make sense of what was happening. "It's the middle of the night. What are you talking about?"

"Kwe. He took my truck. He better hope I don't find him," Kộ said angrily.

"Wait, Kộ. Calm down. Are you sure?" Ts'ı asked as she reached for him.

"Ts'ı, I've had it with him. He's lost all respect," Kộ shouted before barging out of the bedroom, leaving her sitting upright in bed alone with the light on.

Kộ headed straight to Woods's house and banged on the door. By the looks of it, he'd had a party that night or was still partying, with the lingering smell of marijuana escaping under the crack at the bottom of the door and onto the front porch.

"What's going on, brother?" Woods said as he opened the door with one eye open, slightly hunched over, unable to stand up straight.

"I need to borrow your truck," Kǫ̀ said.

"For what?" Woods asked.

"Kwe took off with mine. I need to find him before he wrecks it," Kǫ̀ said impatiently.

"Okay, okay, take it easy, brother. I gotta find the keys." Woods left the door open and walked back into his messy house. Kǫ̀ watched from the doorway as Woods dug into the cracks in the couch for his keys, rolling a random passed-out partygoer on his side.

Kǫ̀ drove around town looking for any sign of his truck but soon ran out of road. The only other place Kwe could be was on the ice road that led out to some of the larger commercial trapping cabins far from town. He didn't think that Kwe would have had the stupidity to drive out of town, let alone travel on the ice road but then again, he hadn't thought his son would steal from him either, so Kǫ̀ decided to check it out to be sure.

Kǫ̀ drove to the end of the ice road that ran parallel to the peninsula a ways out and stopped when he saw fresh tire tracks. The road led out onto one of the off-roads about a twenty-minute drive out, near a small cluster of islands that only the people on the peninsula knew was the best place for trapping mink.

He followed the tracks for a few minutes and looked down at the gas tank.

"Of course, he didn't put gas in it," Kǫ̀ grumbled under his breath and hit the steering wheel when he saw the gage pointing at empty but went on anyway, hoping that it would run on fumes just long enough to get him to the end of the road and back.

It was minus forty, and in his rush Kǫ̀ hadn't dressed for being out so far on the ice road. The roads weren't used often enough to have them regularly maintained, and he knew if he were to get stuck, he would need to walk back in the cold with no help in sight until he reached the shoreline, risking losing a few toes and fingers. Nonetheless, he forged on ahead with a gut feeling to keep going on just a bit further, but around each corner that the small winding road led him down there was no sign of Kwe. He cursed to himself and gripped the steering wheel, about to give up, and then, right out in front of him, under the light of the rising sun circled in a sun dog, was his truck.

Kǫ̀ noticed right away that his truck's front end was stuck in a large snowbank just off the narrow road. As he neared, he could see four shiny black-haired heads in the cab sitting inside the idling truck. Kǫ̀ jumped out of Woods's truck and walk-ran to his own truck.

When Kǫ̀ opened the door, he saw that all four of the kids inside were passed out — why and what from Kǫ̀ couldn't be sure. Little did he know they'd been huffing gas. He reached in and tried to shrug Kwe awake, but he wouldn't budge.

"Kwe?" Kǫ̀ yelled, and one of the kids beside him stirred, slightly startled by his voice. Nelson had trouble but managed to open one eye and when he saw Kǫ̀ he tapped Kwe on the shoulder. Kwe woke up in a daze and saw his father's angry face staring back at him.

"Dad."

Kǫ̀ used the half-filled jerry can he found at their feet to fill up Woods's truck and drive them all back to the peninsula, leaving his own truck behind.

It wouldn't be the last time Kwe would steal a vehicle. He taught himself how to hotwire old makes of unlocked cars after watching too many action movies and soon established the nickname Jack, short for highjack.

After dropping out of high school altogether, Nelson, Kwe and his new girlfriend Coleen, who had been in the same class as Kwe for all of grade school and one of the only girls who was ever nice to him, banded together and stole a car from the only car dealership in town and drove it on the only highway south.

Kwe and Coleen had been dating for only a few short months. He had been too shy to ever speak to her before, but one night after downing a few too many drinks at the same party she was at, they started talking and he ended up telling her all about his life and to his surprise, she actually seemed interested. He shared with her his deepest fears and regrets about not being able to continue with hockey and talked about how he didn't think he could ever live up to the wishes of his father. He confided in her like no one he had ever confided in before, and if that was a girlfriend then he was okay with it.

When they left town soon after, they didn't get very far before crashing the stolen car in the ditch. Nelson had been driving when the car sped out of control and rolled into the ditch upside down. The details of the accident were sparse. Kwe was so traumatized that he wouldn't speak of what happened to Nelson, even when the police questioned him again and again. Kwe never even opened up to Kǫ̀ or Ts'ı about what happened that tragic night, and afterwards, he slipped further into regression, reaching a new low — drug dealing.

After Nelson died, Kwe felt he owed it to his friend to fulfill his dream of going to the big city, and it was there that Kwe got caught up in the gang life and became more distant from his family than ever. He traveled back and forth from the city to Coppertown transporting drugs.

Word got around on the streets of Coppertown fast that Kwe was selling. Over time one of his regular customers, the captain of his old hockey team, came up to Kwe in the back of the local diner where he often hung out and put money down on the table in front of him. Common interests had made the two enemies civil with one another, and when Kwe pushed a gram of cocaine under the table, making the trade, he noticed three men sitting at a small table across from them, watching the exchange go down.

Kwe shoved the money in his pocket and again glanced over at the men while taking a sip of his pop. He felt their eyes on him as the plainclothes police officers stared in his direction. Kwe could tell something wasn't right. In the drug world, there is no such thing as being overly suspicious.

"I gotta take a leak," he told his friends who sat next to him.

Kwe wasted no time and ran to the washroom inside the restaurant and started dumping the drugs into the toilet as beads of sweat rolled down his face. His adrenaline soared with every flush, causing him to work faster, but the toilet didn't seem to flush as fast as Kwe wanted it to, to get rid of the evidence.

He heard metal chairs scraping across the wooden floor, the fast movement of someone getting up quickly and one of his friends yell, "We didn't do nothin'!"

Kwe opened the door just slightly to see his friends getting arrested as the whole restaurant watched the cops in their civilian clothes take them down.

Kwe's so-called friends were brought into the police station, detained and strip-searched. When the police asked them where Kwe was and what he was doing, they told them everything they needed to know to make an arrest.

Being dragged out of his house in handcuffs in the early evening while the neighbourhood came out to see the commotion didn't bother Kwe. It was the looks on his parents' faces that made him hang his head in shame. He would have to spend the rest of his life trying to make it up to them.

His drug-dealing days were over, as short-lived as they were. When his young legal aid lawyer, who showed up to court late with wet hair, requested a lesser sentence, it was denied due to the high-profile gang activity he was involved in and his unwillingness to give details about who was supplying him the drugs. The judge openly made an example out of him, sentencing Kwe to serve a lengthy jail sentence in a maximum-security prison in the south.

As Kwe was led out of the courtroom in handcuffs ready to be transported to cells, he turned around to face his mother with a scared look in his eyes and mouthed the words, “I’m sorry.”

Kǫ̀ hadn’t gone to the sentencing. Ts’ı had to be the one to give him the news when she got home. One look from her and he knew that Kwe wasn’t going to be coming home anytime soon.

Kǫ̀ felt like he no longer knew his son. He didn’t teach him all that he knew just so that he could turn around and throw it all away. He wanted Kwe to be strong and carry on the way of life his father taught him and his father’s father and so on. He’d wanted for Kwe a life of freedom out on the land and was beside himself that his only son had chosen a life completely the opposite.

CHAPTER 19

Įt’ǫ̀a never thought she would ever have the chance to go to college. It was too expensive, and her family wasn’t in the position to save for a higher education like most of the families in Coppertown, but when she was given a full scholarship from Chief and Council after applying on a whim, she couldn’t turn it down. Going to nursing school had been a dream of hers ever since she went with her mom to work at the doctor’s office in the evenings as a little girl. She felt the pressure of having to prove that she was good enough, but it wouldn’t be much different than how she already felt, always having to be on her best behaviour. After Kwe went to jail, most of Įt’ǫ̀a’s time was spent trying to be an exemplary child so that it would take the focus off her brother’s downward spiral.

Although she was afraid to leave home on her own to go to school down south, she was more concerned about having to leave her parents. They weren’t getting any youngęr and she worried they’d be lonely without her, that the same thing might happen to them that happened to Mamia.

Ts’ı was happy that Įt’ǫ̀a had done well in school and was continuing on to college, but Kǫ̀ didn’t understand why she was still going to put herself through school after she already graduated.

“Isn’t twelve years of school good enough?”

“You don’t understand. She needs to keep going.”

Kǫ̀ had his reservations about her going off to college, mostly because he was afraid to lose her to the city.

"The city's dangerous," Kǫ̀ said.

"It's not much different than Coppertown, just bigger, that's all."

"What if she forgets where she's from? What if she forgets about us?" he said.

"Did you forget?"

He shook his head. Times were different. He knew that. This wasn't residential school. Įt'ǫ̀a was not being forced to be in a place she didn't want to be. She was choosing to go.

"Most people would be happy if their kid went off to college, you know," Ts'ı said as they were getting ready to bring Įt'ǫ̀a to the airport.

"Well, I'm not most people."

Ts'ı kissed him on the cheek and rubbed his back as he sat on the edge of the bed in their room.

"What if she doesn't come back?"

"She will. This house might not be a home but we are her home. Besides, she's got to come back and take care of her old dad," Ts'ı teased. "Let's hurry now. We don't want to her to miss her plane."

"Be careful out there in the big city and promise us that you won't ever walk alone at night," Ts'ı said as they stood in line waiting for Įt'ǫ̀a to go through security to catch her plane, her first time flying.

"I know Mom, I won't."

Kǫ̀ stood stoic and rigid at Ts'ı's side, trying to hide his emotions when Įt'ǫ̀a turned to him.

"Dad, it's not like I'm never coming back."

Kǫ̀ looked down at his feet from the other side of the roped aisle. Įt'ǫ̀a knew her dad was struggling to say the right words, to tell her how he felt. She could see through his awkwardness that he didn't want to say goodbye. His only daughter was leaving home to live in the big city, a place he had never been nor ever would venture if he could help it. He didn't have to go there to know that the city was a threat to his entire belief system and now his loved ones too, and he tensed up every time he thought of Įt'ǫ̀a living there alone.

Įt'ǫ̀a hugged her dad, and her mom joined in until they all formed a small circle with the dividing rope between them.

"Me and your father will come see you for Christmas, don't you worry," Ts'ı said. Kǫ̀'s eyebrows wrinkled in confusion; that was news to him.

Įt'ǫ̀a laughed, "Dad, it's okay. I don't expect to see you in the city anytime soon. I'll be home before you know it." She smiled.

Ts'ı visited Įt'ǫ̀a every chance she could, taking the long two-day bus ride to get to the city as she couldn't afford an expensive plane ticket and would just as soon take the bus over flying anyway.

While in the city, Ts'ı soon discovered the bright lights of the casinos and couldn't resist trying her luck. Įt'ǫ̀a and Ts'ı walked into an octagon-shaped casino in the middle of downtown, and Ts'ı was instantly awestruck when she entered the large open room bustling with the sounds of ringing alarm bells as people moved from game to game.

Ts'ı went straight for the biggest, flashiest machine and put in a twenty-dollar bill. Not knowing how to play, she ended up losing within a few seconds. Įt'ǫ̀a tried her hand at the poker table and was dealt a pair of aces right off the bat, winning by fluke. "Beginner's luck," the men around the table said and laughed. They were soon right, in less than a few minutes both Įt'ǫ̀a and Ts'ı were out of money and back at the lobby.

"Mom, as much as I don't want you gambling, I think you should just stick to your scratch tickets."

"Yeah, try telling your father that." Ts'ı smiled. "Let's get out of here before we have nothing left."

CHAPTER 20

It was on those days that he was alone without Ts'ı to keep him company that Kọ̀ missed Kwe and Įt'ọ̀a the most. It was hard for him to believe that they had grown up so fast and both were in the big city, not anywhere near where he expected them to be. Both in an institution. One free and one locked away. Like Mamia, being away from his children caused him to become old too soon, but that wasn't the only thing slowing him down.

It became increasingly difficult for Kọ̀ to make it through to the end of the day at work. He began to make simple mistakes, and it didn't take very long for his supervisor to notice.

"Kọ̀ come see me after your shift," his supervisor told him one day after he had rear-ended one of the work trucks in a minor fender bender. His coughing fits had become so bad that they interfered with almost everything he did.

Kọ̀ knew he was going to be reprimanded. He had been waiting for it. Over the last weeks, he could see his supervisor keeping an extra eye on him, keeping track of his slip-ups, and this one took the cake.

"You wanted to see me," Kọ̀ said as he stood in the doorway after his shift, still wearing his yellow hard hat. His boss's trailer was small, but somehow management was able to squeeze in together once a week and draw up maps of where next to blast.

"Kọ̀, I'm going to have to cut back on your pay."

"I'm already getting paid less than the new guys shovelling the pits and doing twice as much work," Kọ̀ argued and threw his hand in the direction of the gaping hole in the ground just steps from where he stood.

"I know, I know, but you're costing us money. Maybe you should think about hangin' up the old hard hat," the boss said, knocking on his own hat.

"You know what, maybe you're right," Kǫ̀ said to both of their surprise.

"I'm done helping you destroy what's left of this land. I quit." Kǫ̀ took off his hard hat and set it down firmly on a drawing of the tunnels he had worked in day in and day out for too many years to count.

"You quit?" Ts'ı asked in shock.

"I thought you saw this coming. Why are you so surprised?"

"I guess I just thought you'd talk to me about it first."

"Well it happened so fast," he said, avoiding eye contact.

"So what now?" she asked.

"You mean how are we going to afford to live? Ts'ı, we haven't been living, don't you see. All this time we haven't really lived."

Ts'ı didn't speak.

"Listen, we'll be okay. My pension'll kick in soon, the government owes me. Once they start to pay it, we can go make our home on the land like we've always wanted," he said.

Ts'ı was still silent but offered an unenthusiastic shrug.

"That is what you want too, right? To live out on the land?"

Ts'ı still didn't respond.

"Ts'ı?"

"I don't know anymore, Kǫ̀. I'm not like you, I wasn't raised out on the land. I'm getting older. How am I supposed to haul water and do all the things that I've never really done before I started living with you?" she stammered.

"I thought you wanted the same thing," Kǫ̀ said, suddenly

feeling more alone than he'd ever felt in his life, betrayed somehow.

"You never asked me what I wanted Kǫ̀. It's always been about what you've wanted."

Kǫ̀ took a minute to think about it. Was she right? All this time had he not considered what she wanted? He had always just suspected that Ts'ı wanted the same things as him, but now it felt as though Ts'ı was a completely different person.

Kǫ̀ slept on the couch that night. The first time in all their years together that they hadn't slept side by side when under the same roof. He shivered all night. His back and feet couldn't find the warmth that he found when she pressed beside him. They stopped speaking to each other, and in the days ahead an uneasy silence grew between them.

Ts'ı's addiction to buying tickets should have been an indication to Kǫ̀ that she wanted more than what she had. It was true. Ts'ı wanted to come into a windfall of money to be able to afford a new home like the ones up the hill in Coppertown, but she had trouble being honest with Kǫ̀ about how she truly felt, she knew it wasn't what he would have wanted. It wasn't that she didn't want to live out on the land as Kǫ̀ did. She just didn't want to go back to living a life full of long hard days of work. When their home was destroyed, it was traumatic for her having to resort to living in the tent. That winter had been a struggle that she never wanted to endure again.

When Kǫ̀ went into the government office soon after he quit to start the process of claiming his pension, the income assistance officer denied him funding after taking one look at his social insurance profile.

"I'm sorry, sir, but it says here that you have twenty-one thousand and change in arrears with the housing office," the officer said.

"What?" Kǫ̀ spoke so loudly that the other income officers looked over at him in disapproval.

"It says here that you are in debt with the housing corporation and, until it's paid off, we'll have to garnish your wages," the officer repeated.

Kǫ̀ had forgotten all about the last agreement he signed with Walters. He had given up on housing ever helping his family and hadn't been in contact with Walters ever since Chief and Council took over the administrative side of housing. He never did report his income and only paid the base rent while the arrears piled up and the eviction notice fell between the cracks.

As much he didn't want to tell Ts'ı, knowing full well it might just be her breaking point, he knew he had to be honest with her.

"I'm not going to be able to collect a pension for a while. Housing's clawing it back until the arrears are paid off."

To his surprise, Ts'ı wasn't upset; in fact, it sounded like she had a solution.

"Lucy and her family were going through the same thing. Housing was taking their paycheques, but she said housing made them sign their land rights over illegally. Remember when you signed the paper for us to not have to pay the bills anymore?" she asked.

"Yeah, but what does that have to do with anything?"

"It was against the law and we have rights. We can ask them to take it back," she said.

"Sounds too good to be true."

"It's true. Lucy got her house back for a dollar because they got a lawyer. She told them what happened and now they don't have to pay for the house. They own it," she said sounding hopeful.

"But I don't want to own this house. It's worthless to me."

"It wouldn't hurt to go in and talk to Walters and tell him you're going to get a lawyer if they try taking your pension away. He's still there, isn't' he?"

Turns out, Mr. Walters was still there, abusing his authority as always.

"Long time, old friend. You're not looking too well."

Kǫ̀ ignored his sneer and slammed the piece of paper down on the desk, the same paper he signed years ago.

"You know what you are. You're nothing but a greedy bloodsucker. You won't win this time ..." Kǫ̀ began to cough uncontrollably and couldn't finish all that he wanted to say.

"Doesn't look like you got too much fight left in you," Walters said in a taunt.

"I've been fighting my whole life and you know what? I'm getting good at it," Kǫ̀ said and walked out without giving Walters the satisfaction of having the last word.

The second Kǫ̀ left the building Walters yelled out to Nora, "Get rid of all Mr. Collins' files. Burn them if you have to."

Ts'ı noticed that Kǫ̀ had developed a permanent cough before he even realized it for himself, but when she confronted him about it, he refused to go to the doctor.

"You need to see a doctor," Ts'ı urged.

"I'm not going to no doctor," he managed to argue while trying to get his cough under control.

"Įt'ǫ̀a is going to be a nurse one day Kǫ̀. Is that how you are going to think of her too? There's nothing wrong with you going to the doctor."

"Fine I'll go in but only because of Įt'ǫ̀a," he said, wheezing with every exhale.

In all his life, Kǫ̀ had never been to the doctor, not even once, but it got to the point that he was having such a hard time breathing that he had no other choice.

As he sat in the waiting room, he shifted in the hard leather chair and fiddled and folded the napkin he used to cover his mouth and spit into. When they called him in, Ts'ı went too in case he tried to leave out the back door.

"I'll send for some routine bloodwork. You go home now and rest until the lab work comes back," the doctor said after listening to his lungs.

A few days later the doctor called and told them both what both of them weren't prepared to hear.

"Christian, I'm afraid you're going to need to come back in and see me."

"Why? What now? It's nothing you can't tell me over the phone."

"There's no easy way to tell you this, but I'm afraid that you've got cancer. It's progressed to an advanced stage. You've got a few months, maybe a year. Chemotherapy is an option, but you need to be in better health for that to happen and I'm afraid, well …"

Kǫ̀ held the phone far from his ear as the house caved in all around him.

"Christian, you need to let your wife know. If you would have come in sooner maybe things would be different... Christian? Mr. Collins?"

Kǫ̀ slowly put the phone down on the table, missing the receiver.

"I told you. Doctors only ever bring bad news," Kǫ̀ said somberly. Ts'ı had heard it all as she listened behind his shoulder and was already in tears.

"I'm not doing chemo," Kǫ̀ said quietly in his hoarse voice. "Ts'ı," he cleared his throat. "Promise me …"

"Yes?" She cried.

"Don't let me die inside this house." He held her hand firmly in fear, not for himself but for all that he was going to have to leave behind.

Kǫ often swore that the mine would eventually be the death of him, but he didn't think it would happen so soon. He blamed his early death sentence on the house, on the mine, on his own anger.

His mind drifted back to the prophecy his father shared with him years ago. Maybe he had it wrong all this time. Maybe the story of the bison and the muskox was meant for him. That his life would end once the two animals collided on each other's territories.

Soon after he was diagnosed, Kǫ could no longer do simple things that he used to do, like drive, let alone put on his own seatbelt. He couldn't get in his canoe and paddle out to where he wanted to be because he was often too overcome with weakness and fatigue. When he did eat, he had no appetite and could hardly keep anything down.

He began to sleep a lot and with sleep came the nightmares. Even in his sleep, he got no rest, terrorized by the Indian agent banging loudly on his door. Kǫ would open his mouth to tell him to go away but no words would come out. From there he would suddenly morph behind the eyes of the bison watching his relative, the muskox, far off in the distance at the top of the waterfall, struggling to get out of the way of the falling rocks just moments before plunging to its death.

Kǫ didn't want to dream. He didn't want to sleep for fear that he would succumb to the deep sleep, the one he could not wake up from, every time he closed his eyes. He fought slumber just like he fought most everything in his life, with conviction, and for the first time, Kǫ was afraid, not for himself but for what it would be like for his family to have to pick up the pieces after he was gone.

He couldn't bear to have his ghost endlessly walk the floors of the ghastly house with no way out. To leave behind his memory imprisoned in the damp walls, making his presence forever known in the creaky floors, was unthinkable. He had to put things back to the way they were before it was too late.

CHAPTER 21

Kǫ̀ didn't want the kids to know about his health, and Ts'ı tried to respect his wishes. Besides she wouldn't know how to come right out and tell them. She couldn't tell Kwe that his father was terminally ill while he was sitting in a jail cell. There would be nothing he could do, and it would probably make things worse for him. And Įt'ǫ̀a, how could she tell Įt'ǫ̀a her father had cancer while she was in the last year of nursing school? Ts'ı held onto hope that the doctor was wrong, that Kǫ̀ had more time, but the medicine he was given was making him even sicker than he already was, and she felt that he was quickly running out of time. She had to do something. If Mamia were still alive, she'd know what to do to help him, Ts'ı thought. Ts'ı didn't know the first thing about the plant medicine Mamia used, but she knew who might and had to try even if it meant breaking her promise to Kǫ̀.

"Įt'ǫ̀a? Hi. How are you? How's school?" Try as she might to sound upbeat, Ts'ı's voice sounded stuffed up from crying, overwhelmed by having to carry the weight of it all.

"Mom? What's wrong?" Įt'ǫ̀a could tell her mother was upset,

"It's your father … he's not doing so good. He didn't want me to tell you. He doesn't want it to cause problems with your schooling," Ts'ı said with a sniffle, "but I just had to let you know, Įt'ǫ̀a. I'm not sure what to do anymore."

"What? What happened? How bad is it?" Įt'ǫ̀a asked.

"He's not good," she said gravely. "It's the cancer."

Suddenly the distance between them felt further away than ever.

"I'm coming home," Įt'ǫ̀a said, abruptly.

"No. No. Your father was afraid of that. That's why he didn't want me to tell you. You stay and finish your schooling. He's holding on." Ts'ı tried to find the words to calm Įt'ǫ̀a as she tried to hold herself together. "I was hoping you might know what to do. Like what kind of medicines Mamia might have given him if she were still here."

"Mom," Įt'ǫ̀a cried. "I'm coming home. I don't care what he says, I'm coming home." Įt'ǫ̀a hung up the phone, trying to hold in her panicked tears. Įt'ǫ̀a was in the middle of studying for her finals when Ts'ı called but she didn't care. Nothing was as important to her as her father, and she used the rest of her scholarship funds to buy herself the first ticket home.

She knew she was taking a chance on throwing it all away by just picking up and leaving. Her supervisors warned her before she left that not writing her exams would put her back a year —either that or she would have to go to summer school. She would need to rewrite her exams and there was no guarantee her scholarship would last if she put everything on hold, but she couldn't think about that now. She had to be there for her father. What if he were to take a turn for the worse? Not being there might mean she wouldn't have the chance to say goodbye. That already happened once. She couldn't let it happen again, she thought.

Įt'ǫ̀a was so young when Mamia taught her about traditional medicine; having been healed after being gravely sick herself, she knew there was a teaching in each and every plant. Mamia had given her insight into an entire belief system that was capable of healing nearly every ailment known to humans. She might just be able to help her dad if she could remember how to wake that knowledge up and out of her sleeping memory.

In nursing school, Įt'ǫ̀a was taught the opposite of what Mamia taught her. She learned how to poke and prod, stick needles into arms and draw blood, use thermometers to test for fevers and listen to heartbeats with cold instruments. Not once was she asked to hold someone's hand to console them when they were scared. She was taught not to show empathy, only to keep track of symptoms on a check board. She was to only administer drugs to bandage the problem, not cure it. There was no compassion in the system she was learning in, and absolutely no talk of natural traditional medicines was tolerated.

Upon returning to the North, it would take Įt'ǫ̀a a few days to get used to the cold again. She was cold the entire plane ride, not having dressed for the winter she was headed back into.

It was the last flight of the day and well past midnight when she arrived tired and chilled. After grabbing her bags from the slow-moving carousal, the line-up outside for a taxi was long.

Most of the travellers were only in town on a work trip. Business was booming in Coppertown since diamonds had been found, gold had become a thing of the past. The businessmen and women wore black suits and pulled around their briefcases on wheels while Įt'ǫ̀a carried a secondhand suitcase next to them and wore her comfiest clothes, her hair up in a lose bun.

"I only have a ten and some change," Įt'ǫ̀a said when she saw the meter getting closer to ten dollars in big red numbers hanging from an old alarm clock contraption on the dash of the taxi.

"You don't have enough to get all the way home?" The taxi driver nearly slammed on the brakes, stopping in the middle of the lonely road when he found out he was being short-changed."I didn't think it was going to be this much," Įt'ǫ̀a explained desperately.

"You get out here then. Too many kids like you always ditching cabs. Get out," he said and rolled the car to a stop in the middle of the small bridge connecting the peninsula to Coppertown.

Įt'ǫ̀a was too tired to argue. She gave him the last of her money and took her outdated suitcase out of the trunk without his help. She walked the rest of the way home in the dark, dropping her heavy belongings every once in a while to catch a break and warm her cold fingers nipped by the night's cool air. By the time she arrived on her doorstep, she was exhausted.

Ts'ı was already awake waiting when she heard Įt'ǫ̀a's footsteps on the stairs leading up to the house, followed by the sound of her daughter's old brown leather suitcase bumping against the stairs. Ts'ı got up slowly from the bed, trying not to wake Kǫ̀. She still hadn't told him that Įt'ǫ̀a was coming home.

Kǫ̀ opened his eyes when he heard someone coming up the stairs and tried to get up to check but his body was stiff. The more he lay in his bed the harder it was for him to get up.

"Do you hear that?" Kǫ̀ asked.

"I'll go see what it is. Don't worry yourself," Ts'ı said.

She walked out into the dark living room and opened the front door to see Įt'ǫ̀a struggling to get up the stairs.

"Mom," she cried.

"Sshh. Try not to wake your father. He still doesn't know yet," Ts'ı said as she helped lift her bag.

"Who are you talking to? Don't know what?" Kǫ̀ had managed to make his way up and out of bed on his own and met them at the door as he leaned on the wall for support.

"Hi Dad," Įt'ǫ̀a said and ran to him with a big hug. He was so fragile that she had to hug him gently. He swam inside the old checkered flannel jacket he got from her one year for Christmas, his skin clammy.

"Įt'ǫ̀a. How'd you get here? You're done school already?" He felt delirious. Had he missed a huge chunk of time?

"No Dad. I came home to see you."

Kǫ̀ used up what energy he had to give a slight smile and shake his head. He put his hand on her shoulder for balance, and Ts'ı tucked under his other arm and they both helped him back to bed.

Įt'ǫ̀a wasted no time going out on the land to gather medicines.

"I don't want my children to save me. It's supposed to be the other way around," Kǫ̀ said faintly to Ts'ı behind the closed door of their bedroom after Įt'ǫ̀a left for the day. Ts'ı looked out the window at Įt'ǫ̀a wondering where she was off to after putting a double layer of socks on Kǫ̀'s feet to keep him warm since his circulation wasn't flowing from not moving.

Įt'ǫ̀a knew not to go close to the vicinity of the mine to forage for anything. She heard too many stories of people getting sick from harvesting plants and berries near the site. Even smelling the flowers would be enough to cause someone to have to take bed rest for a couple of days.

Įt'ǫ̀a didn't go as far as she had wanted to out of fear that she might get lost, but she went far enough to feel the sense of complete solitude. She went up river until the water was clear enough to see the bottom. It was there that she floated, taking her time snapping cattails, knowing that the insides of their velvet brown cover were good for numbing pain.

It was early spring and the willows were just starting to bloom but the green on the leaves had not yet budded. She'd have to come back in summer to pick newborn wildflowers and spruce tips, but for now she had enough to start with. She thanked

Mamia when she saw a large piece of tłeet'ah within arm's reach on one of the tall birch trees just before turning around and heading for home.

When she docked the canoe near the tłeet'ah tree, she saw fresh bear droppings on the trail in front of her and looked around to make sure the path was clear, but as she reached for the tłeet'ah she didn't notice a medium-sized black bear meandering around eating berries in the trees nearby. The bear saw her first and instantly saw her as a threat. It charged at her to protect itself, swiping at her with its long claws from a few feet away on its hind legs. Standing as tall as her, it was a young bear, but it was fast, lean and hungry, having slept most of the winter. Įt'ǫ̀a didn't quite know what to do, not having encountered a bear up close before. She didn't have anything to ward it off other than the small pocketknife she used to saw off thick tangled pieces of nàedı in the mud near the shore of the river.

Then she remembered that Mamia burned birch bark to ward off bears. "Sah don't like the smell of this," Mamia explained as they went on their hikes, but Įt'ǫ̀a had no time to light a match. The bear scurried up the tree in front of her as if it was climbing spiral stairs and turned to get a good look at her — looking down from above. It bobbed its nose up and down sniffing at the air around her, the tip of its nose moving like it had a life of its own. Įt'ǫ̀a tried to back away slowly but the young bear pawed at her again. Not sure of what to do next, Įt'ǫ̀a stood as still as can be, hoping it would leave her alone. It was the only thing she could do as it most certainly would outrun her if she tried making her way back to the canoe.

The standoff lasted quite some time as the bear tried to decide whether she was an imminent threat. Just when it made up its mind to attack, Įt'ǫ̀a saw an arrow zip through the trees, scoring the bear in the eye, leaving it in a heap at her feet right before it had the chance to sink its teeth into her.

Įt'ǫ̀a looked around to see where the arrow came from and out of the trees came a boy, not much older than her, with long dark hair hanging in front of his eyes and muddy bare feet.

"Close one," he said moving towards her. Flinging his bow and arrow over his shoulder, he knelt and put his hand on the bear's belly to check if it was still breathing.

"Where did you …? How did you …?" Įt'ǫ̀a's heart was racing.

"I've been tracking this guy for a while. His mother left him too young. He's been coming into our camp. He's got a taste for human food now; it wasn't a choice really."

"Where's your shoes?" was all Įt'ǫ̀a could come up with in response.

"I like to make things more challenging."

"The name's Elvis."

"The bear?

"No, my name's Elvis." He laughed.

"Oh."

"Like the singer," Elvis hinted but Įt'ǫ̀a didn't catch on.

"You know, Elvis." He pretended to play air guitar for a moment and shook a leg.

"You ain't nothin but a hound dog," he sang terribly.

"Oh, okay yeah." Įt'ǫ̀a smiled awkwardly feeling embarrassed for him.

"What do they call you?"

"Įt'ǫ̀a," she said.

"Like the flower."

"Yeah."

"Nice name."

An awkward silence filled the air between them above the cadaver.

"What are you doing out here anyway?" he asked.

"I'm just gathering some plants."

"What's going to happen to it now?" Ts'ı asked.

"Probably give him away to someone that needs it. My family doesn't eat bear. Yours?"

"No." Įt'ǫ̀a shook her head. Mamia taught Įt'ǫ̀a that only certain families were allowed to consume bear. Come to think of it, Mamia told her once that bear was a very powerful medicine because it was a spirit animal. "*Sah weɂek'a wet'à tada łǫ kaɂa nayejìa ha dìle.*"

Įt'ǫ̀a thought out loud, "But ... I might be able to make use of it." She couldn't believe what she was committing to.

"Alright then, let's load him up," Elvis said and helped Įt'ǫ̀a carry the bear, which weighed more than the both of them together, into the bow of the canoe by its limbs.

"Well thanks for saving me, I guess?" She wasn't sure what to say as she got into the boat.

"Yeah anytime." He laughed. "I mean, hopefully I won't have to save you again."

"Yeah."

Įt'ǫ̀a got into her canoe and tried to push off, but the bear weighed down the canoe until it touched the bottom of the shallow shoreline. She felt a strong push freeing the canoe into the water and turned to thank Elvis but he was already gone.

"Where did you say you got it from?" Kǫ̀ asked again.

"Someone named Elvis. He sort of saved me," Įt'ǫ̀a said, as Kǫ̀ was still trying to grapple with how the whole surreal scenario played out after Įt'ǫ̀a told him there was a black bear in the canoe.

"What kind of a name is Elvis anyway?" Kǫ̀ asked.

"Mamia used to love Elvis," Ts'ı recalled.

"What are you going to do with it?" Kǫ̀ asked while trying to hold off a coughing fit.

"I'm going to try to make nàedı for you." Įt'ǫ̀a smiled.

"Don't let the flesh and bones touch the ground," Kǫ̀ said seriously before retreating to his bed for a rest.

"Should we call Woods and ask him to come help?" Ts'ı asked gently.

Kǫ̀ nodded, "But tell him it has to be done soon or the meat will go bad."

As Į̀t'ǫ̀a and Ts'ı waited for Woods to come to the house and help cut up the meat, they took it upon themselves to carry the bear carcass into the yard, where Kǫ̀ had his hunting tent set back up, its torn canvas ripped and flailing in the warm wind.

"How are we going to do this?" Į̀t'ǫ̀a asked.

"We'll skin it the same way we would a moose or a caribou." Ts'ı got to work pulling at the bear's fur to get a good enough grasp to separate it from the fatty layer of tissue underneath. Once completely skinned, the bear looked more human than animal, and it scared Į̀t'ǫ̀a to look at it for too long, knowing it had been either the bear or her.

When it was time to cut into the meat, Woods was ready with an electric saw, which Kǫ̀ would have frowned upon if he had seen it, but Woods's excuse was "it's fast and makes a clean cut through the bone."

"Just make sure you don't let it touch the ground," Ts'ı reminded him.

They worked on top of a plastic fold-up table covered with flattened cardboard boxes, cutting up the bear fat and joints into small sections to be put into baggies to freeze and give away to those who were accustomed to eating bear.

Ts'ı helped by hacking away at the thicker pieces of bone with an axe while Į̀t'ǫ̀a sat inside the teepee and de-haired the hide, careful not to be disrespectful to the spirit of the animal by covering her nose, but the strong smell was something she wasn't used to and she couldn't help but go outside every so often for fresh air.

Once all the fur was off, Ts'ı and Į̀t'ǫ̀a wrapped the hide

around a thick sturdy stick and used all their strength to twist it into a ball to get the remaining water out of it, dripping the liquid into a cast iron pot. They would later render the fat over a fire until it became a thick consistency, good enough to use as a salve but also as a thick cough medicine that they hoped would give Kǫ̀ the strength of the bear.

It took the two of them to stretch the corners of the bear hide afterwards and they nailed each point of the hide on four equally sized trees that were bound together at the ends to form a perfect square. Over the next few weeks, they would work at shaving the flesh and fat off the hide, scraping it with the flat end of a smoothed caribou bone until it was soft and their hands were blistered.

When the heavy work of preparing the sah was done, Įt'ǫ̀a ground up the dried plants in the kitchen with Ts'ı. They stirred, mixed and strained until the broth was ready to be poured into a tea and sprinkled it with dry powdery spruce gum.

Everything they did from start to finish was in ceremony. With Kǫ̀ in their hearts and thoughts, a powerful medicine was made that he would drink throughout the days with what little food he could stomach in hopes that he would get well again.

CHAPTER 22

The doctor wouldn't come right out and say that Kǫ̀ was in remission, but they all knew it to be true. Before Įt'ǫ̀a came home, Ko's health was rapidly declining; now he seemed to be holding steady. His tumor may have been shrinking, but they couldn't know for sure because Kǫ̀ refused to go through any more tests.

In only a short time, Kǫ̀'s energy had returned to the point that he was able to get around on his own again without a struggle. This gave him just enough energy to do what he knew he needed to do, what he had longed for most of his life, to fulfill his dream of building a house in the bush. But first, he needed to make sure that Įt'ǫ̀a followed hers.

"You have to go back and finish school Įt'ǫ̀a," he said to her as she and Ts'ı sat outside their house in the summer heat, taking a break from scraping a caribou hide with the flat curved end of their trusted caribou bones.

"I can't," she said as she swatted the flies away that were attracted to the strong smell of wet animal skin, which had been soaked in caribou brain to make it soft and malleable.

"What do you mean, you can't?" Kǫ̀ asked.

"Since I left before exams," she said, "they won't fund me anymore but it's okay; it's just school. It's not important anyway. I already know what to do. I knew how to fix you up good, didn't I?" Įt'ǫ̀a laughed and scratched her nose with the inside of her elbow, the white fluff off the hide making her itchy.

Kǫ̀ wasn't going to accept that she was giving up so easily. He took measures to find out when the next Chief and Council meeting was and demanded to be on the agenda. When it was his turn to talk, he walked up to the large round table made to look like a drum, where the Chief and Council sat, and began to make the case for Įt'ǫ̀a. But he was out of practice and it was difficult for him to speak loud enough for everyone to hear.

"I'm here tonight to ask you to make an exception for my daughter. She quit school to help me get better and now I'm nearly back to health. She needs your help to go back to school and finish what she started," he said.

"I'm sorry but it was stated in the policy that there's a probationary period after someone quits school," the councilor with the portfolio for education said. He couldn't be any older than Įt'ǫ̀a herself, Kǫ̀ thought.

"Besides she took the money and ran off with it," another council member piped in.

"Not to mention your son was selling drugs in our community," said another one.

"Shame on you, shame on all of you. You're supposed to be helping the people, not making their lives harder," Kǫ̀ rebutted.

"That's enough, Kǫ̀. We've made our decision. There's nothing we can do to help you or your daughter any further until her probation is over," the Chief echoed.

"I'm going to find a way to get that money she needs to go back," Kǫ̀ said to Ts'ı later that evening as they were getting into bed.

"If there's one thing I know for sure about you Kǫ̀, is you never give up. I love you for that," Ts'ı said.

"I'll break into the bank if I have to," he said seriously.

"Kǫ̀, don't talk like that," Ts'ı said.

"It's all stolen money anyway. The bank, the government, housing; they're all in on it together, profiting off us, off the land."

At this point, Ts'ı wouldn't put it past him to pull such a stunt. "I see you're back to your old self," she said. "Just promise me you won't be robbing banks anytime soon." She kissed him on the cheek before turning out the light.

The next day, Ts'ı went out and bought a scratch ticket and made a promise to God that it would be the last one she ever bought if only she could just win enough to help Įt'ǫ̀a. She prayed that she be forgiven for making such a bargain with God. "I just don't see any other way," she whispered.

She scratched the ticket with her eyes closed, hoping her family might have some luck just once, but when she opened her eyes and scanned the numbers her heart sank. It was the same as every other time, except the rare occasions where she won up to ten, sometimes twenty dollars, and a huge feeling of letdown flooded her body. She double-checked, even triple-checked, to make sure that she wasn't looking at the numbers wrong.

She brought the ticket to the cashier to run it through the machine. They played tug of war for a few seconds until she finally let go only to see the cashier scan it and rip it in half.

"Better luck next time, lady."

"There won't be a next time," Ts'ı said. "Thanks anyway." Kǫ̀ was right. She was done with spending her hard-earned money on a game that was set up to make her think she had a winning chance.

"Mom? Can you come here?" Įt'ǫ̀a was behind the house looking into the water at something when she saw her mom coming up the drive and hollered.

"What is it?" Ts'ı asked, meeting her at the water's edge.

"Woods just came and dropped off a bunch of caribou hides."

They both looked down at the hides that had been tossed into the cold summer lake water to make it easier to get the fur off them.

"Wow there must be at least ten in there," Ts'ı said.

"He gave us a bunch of hind quarters and back straps too. They're in the house on garbage bags ready to be cut up. We'll be up all night making dry meat," Įt'ǫ̀a said.

"That's odd of him. He's never been so generous before," Ts'ı said as a cold breeze blew off the lake and made the hair on her arms stand up.

Come to think of it, Ts'ı noticed that Woods's skidoos and boat were parked in the driveway on his trailer when she got home too.

When the police came by the house that same day, her questions were answered.

"Are you the next of kin of Woodrow Martin?" the officer asked Ts'ı when she answered the door in fear of what the police were doing there.

"He's my brother-in-law, why? Is everything okay?"

"I'm sorry to tell you that he's passed away. We got a call and found him this morning in his home, deceased," the officer said and handed her a yellow envelope with Woods's house keys.

"How … how did he die?" Ts'ı asked sadly.

Įt'ǫ̀a came up to the door behind Ts'ı and listened.

"We believe it to be self-inflicted. I'm sorry that's all the information I can give you right now. If you and your husband come down to the detachment, we can give you more information."

It all made sense, the giving away of things, Ts'ı thought.

"For now, you might want to go over and collect his personal belongings. Housing has been informed and will be emptying out the unit," the officer said without apologizing for their sudden tragic loss.

"Thank you, officer. We will do that," Ts'ı said and shut the door.

"It wasn't supposed to be this way," Kǫ̀ said in guilt. "I should have been there for him."

"You couldn't have known."

Kǫ̀ looked up at Ts'ı, his eyes bloodshot.

"I had a brother I didn't even take the time to get to know," Kǫ̀ said.

Ts'ı was at a loss of what to say.

"Did you know I saw him a few days ago? He was on the street downtown and I drove on by. Just drove right past. He saw me too. He looked me right in the eye and you know what, Ts'ı? I didn't even smile. I acted like I didn't know him. I didn't even stop." Kǫ̀ was so angry at himself that he wanted to punch his fist through the cheap drywall.

"How'd he do it, Ts'ı? How could he? What did they do to him at that godforsaken school?"

"He'd been drinking a lot too. It was a lot of things. We can never really know how someone is feeling inside."

"Don't. Don't you dare stick up for that damn school. That's what did it. He didn't even know his own name, Ts'ı. Just like you, he didn't even know his own name. They took it from him just like they took away everything else. They took away who he was."

Kǫ̀'s tears eventually tired him out and he fell asleep sitting up on the couch. He blamed himself for not doing enough, for not taking his brother under his wing. He was too busy worrying about his own struggles to stop and think that Woods might have been fighting his own battles too, suffering in silence and trying to drown the pain by drinking.

After Woods was laid to rest next to his mother, Kǫ̀ gave away all his brother's expensive equipment, his boat, skidoos, tools to those in need and burned what was left of his clothing and other belongings to help his spirit return to Creator.

Kǫ̀ heard the whispers in the community. He was well aware of what the church's beliefs were around suicide, but he flat out refused to believe it. He lit a candle and said a prayer to Creator to help his brother find his way back home.

CHAPTER 23

"Are you sure, Dad?" Įt'ǫ̀a asked for the hundredth time.

"He wanted you to have it. Now go and get that education of yours. You'll be the best damn doctor there is," he said proudly.

"Nurse, Dad, nurse," she corrected.

"Just promise you'll come and check on your old dad every once in a while," he said with a smile.

It turned out that Woods had come into a lump sum of money through a residential school settlement before he died. Ts'ı found a large stack of money tucked away in the back of his closet when she was cleaning out his unit. At first, she thought it might have been money made from drug dealing or bootlegging but when she read the letter, the instructions were clearly laid out. It was to go to Įt'ǫ̀a, and it was just enough for her to go back and finish what she started.

"And Kǫ̀, go build that damn cabin of yours once and for all I know you'll make it a home," the letter read.

"What about you? Are you going to be okay?" Įt'ǫ̀a asked her dad.

"I'm stronger than ever, thanks to you."

It was true. The medicine Įt'ǫ̀a gave him each day helped him feel good enough to get back out on the land. Kǫ̀ took his time gathering and prepping what materials he would need to finish the job. The further he went, the stronger he felt. The energy under his feet helped him trudge on. He knew where he needed to go. It was the only place that felt right in his heart. The place of the sacred tree, Ts'ı's homeland, and although she may not share the same dream as him, he still hung on to hope that she would change her mind once she saw what he had in store.

One morning, as Kǫ̀ was gearing up to head out, he heard footsteps walking up behind him and thought maybe it was Ts'ı bringing him a lunch before he set out, but when he turned to see who it was, he was in shock.

"Hi Dad. They, uh, let me out on good behaviour," Kwe said with a look of remorse, standing in front of his father, waiting for what seemed like forever for him to say something, anything. It had already been too long.

Neither Kǫ̀ nor Ts'ı had seen or spoken to Kwe since he'd been sentenced. Kwe cancelled his mother's visits whenever she tried to see him when in the city with Įt'ǫ̀a, too ashamed to have to talk to his mother behind glass.

It had been years since Kǫ̀ had seen his son, but Kwe didn't look any different to him; he was still a boy in Kǫ̀'s eyes. Kǫ̀ on the other hand had aged.

"Dad?" All that Kwe wanted was for his father to forgive him.

Kǫ̀ walked up to Kwe and rested a heavy hand on his shoulder. "It's good to see you."

"I'm sorry, Dad." He burst into tears.

"I know. It's no use looking back now. Just do what you can today to make things right."

And Kwe did as he was told. He set out with his father that same day and every day after that, helping to rebuild what was taken from them all those years ago, and in doing so he slowly started learning the teachings that his father had tried to show him ever since he was young. Kwe began to understand that Creator and the land were one and the same and the land was the only place where he could go to know himself.

Some days, Kǫ̀ was too overcome with sickness to get out of bed, so Kwe would go on without him. In witnessing his father's strength and perseverance throughout his lifetime, Kwe saw the significance of what it meant to his father to be able to rebuild their lives. It wasn't about going back into the past. It was about reclaiming, it was about never giving up, and by the end of the summer, they managed to build a humble log home that was more than Kǫ̀ could have ever imagined.

"Now I just need to convince your mother to come live in it," he said with a nervous laugh.

"She's gonna love it," Kwe said reassuringly but Kǫ̀ wasn't so sure.

Ts'ı hadn't been back to her homeland in so long that she had no idea what to expect when Kǫ̀ held her hand and helped her out of the boat when they arrived on shore.

"I already made up my mind about this Kǫ̀," Ts'ı said softly when he pulled the boat up to the spot where he planned on building a dock. "I don't need to see it," Ts'ı said, standing tall on the flat rock like the large ts'ı straight out in front of them in the distance.

"You don't?" Kǫ̀ asked sadly choking back his words.

She shook her head with a smile. "No. So this is home then, is it?"

Kǫ̀ let out a big sigh of relief and held her hand tight.

Before shutting the door of the housing unit behind him for good, Kǫ̀ ripped out the old woodstove that he found at the dump the year their power was turned off and brought it with him. It was the only thing in the house that was of any use after all those years.

Word spread throughout the community that Kǫ̀ had built a home in the bush, and people came out to visit, bringing housewarming gifts, mostly food to help Ts'ı focus on caring for Kǫ̀.

Soon enough people on the peninsula started reclaiming their land, too. And before Kǫ̀' returned to the spirit world, he was surrounded by a community that helped each other and shared once again. One by one, they overturned their forced dependency on government housing and lived completely on the land. And even though they still had to somewhat incorporate the modern world into their lifestyle, they did so on their own terms, using solar, wind and other green technologies that were in alignment with their ancient principles of caring for the land and water and living off natural resources sustainably.

In his last days, Kǫ̀ was visited by the Indian agent in his sleep. It was the same recurring dream he always had, but this time when he opened his mouth to say something, he was finally able to speak. Ko couldn't hear the words he spoke, but the Indian agent had a shocked look on his face and turned to leave.

Before winter fell that year, Kǫ̀ was finally at peace, knowing he had been able to return to the land. He spent those last precious moments with his family in the house that was built with love and lifelong determination. As the light burned bright from the woodstove under the window that faced the lake, the soft sounds of Elvis's gospel played in the background on low and the glow of the fire matched the feeling in his heart as he looked out at a perfect view of the sunset.

Before his body was given back to the earth, covering him like a blanket, Ts'ı placed the pieces of their shared broken acorn in his hand. She was proud of Kǫ̀ for the man he was and all he had done for his family. Not once had he given up trying to mend the broken pieces of their lives, and it gave her comfort to know that before he left the world he felt complete.

Kwe returned to the waterfall after his father's burial, to the same place they saw the muskox. It was there that Kwe saw the bison and the muskox standing on either side of the roaring waters. In a quiet resolve, both animals slowly nodded and turned away from each other and went their separate ways.

Kǫ̀ was a great man who loved his family and loved the land. He reclaimed his sovereignty and brought truth to his name.

His name is Kǫ̀ and his name means home.

O Great Spirit, whose voice I hear in the winds,
and whose breath gives life to all the world, hear me.
I am small and weak.
I need your strength and wisdom.
Let me walk in beauty and let my eyes ever behold
the red and purple sunset.
Make my hands respect the things you have made.
Make my ears sharp to hear your voice.
Make me wise so that I may understand the things
you have taught your people.
Let me learn the lessons that you have hidden in every leaf and rock.
I seek strength, not to be greater than my brother,
but to fight my greatest enemy – myself.
Make me always ready to come to you
with clean hands and straight eyes.
So when life fades, as the fading sunset,
my spirit may come to you without shame.

— Author unknown,
translated by Lakota Sioux Chief Yellow Lark in 1887

ACKNOWLEDGMENTS

Mahsi cho to Beverley Rach for once again for giving me the opportunity to publish with Roseway and providing me with the supports that I needed.

Special thanks to everyone who entrusted me with their stories of injustice in the housing system.

Mary Rose Sundberg with Goyatiko Language Centre, mahsi cho for working on the translations in our Dene Tłı̨chǫ language in Denendeh.

Kaitlin Littlechild, it was great having you on board for the editing process. It was important that this work be edited by an Indigenous editor, and I am grateful to the Indigenous Editors Association for recommending you for the project; your professionalism is unmatched. Brenda Conroy, mahsi cho for doing the final touches and finding small important details for fixing.

Odette, you are an amazing colleague in the world of freelancing and I hope to share works with you until we run out of things to write about. Mahsi cho for sharing with me your birth stories.

Richard Van Camp, my fellow northern author, mahsi cho for taking an early look at the manuscript and giving me tips on how to add more dialogue. Also mahsi cho for encouraging me to keep writing when I wasn't sure what next step to take after *Northern Wildflower* was published.

My life partner Brian, mahsi cho for supporting me in my writing and being my biggest fan.

Mahsi cho to all my friends and family who were there with

me in the beginning stages of drafting the manuscript and for all your support along the way.

Kilala Lelum, mahsi cho for giving me the inspiration to incorporate traditional Indigenous midwifery into an occupation for Mamia. You are doing wonderful things for the Downtown Eastside of Vancouver — healing the mother wounds.

Mahsi cho to West Vancouver Public Library for giving me the opportunity to use the Climate writing residency to finish the ending of this book in a way that focuses on the issue of climate change to show that tradition and technology can complement each other.

Mahsi cho to Keepers of the Circle for bringing together a group dedicated to addressing the housing crisis in Indigenous communities across Turtle Island.